D0813697

Sacri-
ficial
Smoke

Jan Fridegård

Offerrök
Volume 3 in the Holme Trilogy
Translated, with a foreword
and notes, by Robert E. Bjork
University of Nebraska Press
Lincoln and London

Originally published
as *Offerrök*
in the *Trilogin om*
trälen Holme,
copyright © 1949 by
Aase and Stefan Fridegård
Translation, foreword,
and notes copyright
© 1991 by Robert E. Bjork
All rights reserved
Manufactured in the
United States of America
The paper in this book
meets the minimum
requirements of
American National Standard
for Information Sciences –
Permanence of Paper for
Printed Library Materials,
ANSI Z39.48–1984.
Library of Congress
Cataloging-in-Publication Data
Fridegård, Jan, 1897–1968.
[Offerrök. English]
Sacrificial Smoke
Offerrök/
by Jan Fridegård ;
translated, with
a foreword and notes
by Robert E. Bjork. p. cm. –
(Volume 3 in the Holme trilogy)
(Modern Scandinavian
literature in translation)
Bibliography: p.
ISBN 0-8032-1981-4 (alk. paper)
ISBN 0-8032-6872-6 (pbk.)
I. Bjork, Robert E., 1949– .
II. Title.   III. Title: Offerrök.
IV. Series.   V. Series:
Fridegård, Jan, 1897–1968.
Trilogin om trälen Holme.
English ; v. 3.
PT9875.F7880313 1990
839.7'372 – dc20
89-4916 CIP

I am deeply grateful to Steven C. Spronz, Esq.,
without whose timely and generous help
this translation would not have been published.

Robert E. Bjork

Contents

Foreword

Sacrificial Smoke is the final volume in a trilogy of historical novels by the Swedish author Jan Fridegård (1897–1968). Fridegård was born into a poor working-class family of seven in an area of south-central Sweden rich with Viking artifacts. As a result, he developed a passion for two things: the plight of poor, oppressed working people and the Viking period of Swedish history. The three novels about a ninth-century Viking thrall named Holme and his wife, Ausi, reflect both passions. The first of the novels, *Land of Wooden Gods* (*Trägudars land*, 1940),[1] chronicles Holme's strug-

---

1. Translated, with an afterword and notes, by Robert E. Bjork (Lincoln: University of Nebraska Press, 1989).

gle against his enemies, especially his former chieftain owner, from whom he escapes and who is eventually killed in battle; his successful attempts to save Ausi and their daughter from death or enslavement; and his establishment of himself as a respected blacksmith in a flourishing trade center. It also begins the story of the clash between paganism and Christianity in Sweden and ends with the threat of renewed incursions of Christian missionaries and foreign trade looming on the horizon.

The second volume of the trilogy, *People of the Dawn* (*Grynings-folket*, 1944),[2] takes up where the first leaves off, continuing the saga of Holme and his struggle against his oppressors, primarily his former owner's wife and her brother Geire – a powerful Viking warrior who rapes Ausi – but also the adherents of Christianity, who consider Holme their most awesome foe. By the end of *People of the Dawn*, Holme has led an uprising of slaves against their masters, has killed Geire, and has had to flee to the forests once more to save himself and his family. Sixteen years after escaping their owner in *Land of Wooden Gods*, Holme and Ausi find themselves in exile once more. *Sacrificial Smoke* concludes the story of Holme's exile and develops the account of the increasingly bloody strife between the pagan darkness and the Christian light.

2. Translated, with a foreword and notes, by Robert E. Bjork (Lincoln: University of Nebraska Press, 1990).

Sacri-
ficial
Smoke

Just before sunrise, Holme crawled out of the cave. Ausi and Tora were still sleeping on the moss bed inside, but before they fell asleep, he had forbidden them to leave the cave until he returned. He suspected that the forest would be scoured during the next few days and that this time his enemies wouldn't give up before he was captured or dead.

The gray dew was shimmering on the grassy slope and the spring down below was murmuring just as it had before. The air was cool, the sky clear. By midday, it would be like summer — warm with air so clear you could see the woods and hills in the endless distance. That's how the two days before had been.

Holme closed up the cave with some dry branches before leaving. As he did so, he thought it strange that no wolf, fox, or badger had taken over the cave during his long absences. But maybe the smell of man had lingered on and scared them away.

He had never before walked through the forest without knowing exactly where he was going or what he was doing. He had fought for slaves' rights for a long time, but everything had turned sour. Hardly a single thrall had been freed – or stayed free; many of them had been slaughtered like dogs or hunted through the forest like wild boars as he had been. Whoever finally killed him would be famous.

From old habit, Holme walked toward the settlement where he had spent his youth as a thrall. He had been overseer there, too, for a short time. The men chasing him couldn't have gotten there so early in the morning. He could expect them first around midday. Maybe he could find something at the settlement that could be useful to him either in the cave or during his escape. Everyone in the area knew Holme and his family. He could never again hunt openly in the woods, or fish in the coves, or exchange goods without being recognized, then captured or killed by the chieftain's men. Like an outlaw or an animal, he would be forced to keep hidden during the day and seek food for himself and his family during the dark of night.

At sunrise, he was standing and looking out over the abandoned settlement. Some shocks of grain were still lying where they had been blown over, and the yellowish-gray stubble was glowing among them. The air was awash with dew and crystal clear – from where he stood at the forest's edge he could see a small rat scampering here and there among the sheaves. A light morning mist hung above the cool autumn water in the cove down below, and a couple of coots were gliding like black dots through it.

A few days earlier the settlement had been full of life and laughter, but now it was silent and deserted. A number of slaves who had believed in freedom and the future were now lying beneath the earth outside town, killed and then buried without provisions for their journey, without tools or weapons for the life after death. No one would avenge them, no one would be punished or ordered to pay compensation to their relatives. Thralls lived without the benefit of the law, beyond the provenance of the assembly, which protected freemen.

Though he fought it, Holme felt the old bitterness rising. But there was nothing to do now but run or keep hidden. He still wasn't sure which he would do. The great unknown forests were still beckoning to him. They were unpopulated, and if there were any people in them at all, they were being hunted too, just like him. But the old problem was still there: Ausi could not tolerate the solitude for long. She was different from him and his daughter. She would pine and dream with a sickness even her Christ couldn't cure. On the contrary, He and His appointed priest had given the sickness to her.

Holme walked past the smithy in the rocks and picked up a little-birch bark box with various kinds of tools in its compartments. He would need the tools if he was going to build a house in some isolated place.

The sheaves of grain were swarming with tiny gray sparrows that looked like rats peeping out here and there in the yellow straw. In the chieftain's day the children thralls had always guarded the grain and scared the birds away from the fields. They had been forced to get up with the sun and run around the fields, waving their arms, yelling and throwing stones. But now the sparrows were unmolested. They flew away with a roar of wings when

5

Holme approached the field while the field rats moved fitfully and constantly among the shocks.

The wooden god's stone was empty, but there was a dark clump of wood lying on the slope. Someone had knocked the harvest god over, and Holme wasn't sure who. It couldn't have been him. He walked down to examine the god more closely. The rain had washed most of the soot from the fire off, so gray wood was peeping through now. The god lay on his back, a spider web, gray with fine dewdrops, over his face.

Holme stood there looking at him for a long time, and for the first time he was moved by a wooden god. This one had been at the settlement long before he had; it had seen a great deal and had survived the ravages of the fire, just like him. There might be something to the god after all.

But who had knocked him off his stone, Holme wondered again. He remembered that the thralls had put him up there before starting to harvest the grain. Maybe a moose or a wild boar was scratching itself against the stone and pushed it over. He didn't think that any Christian, who would be provoked by the god, had passed by there recently.

Holme picked up the heavy clump of wood and put it back in place, wondering why as he did so. It might be that he felt it belonged there and that its absence would be noticed. Or maybe he did it to annoy the Christian chieftain, who would surely come after him with his riders that day. Another possibility occurred to him. He had never been in a worse situation, and maybe he should ask the charred wooden god for help. He might still be able to do something for an old acquaintance.

The little hut stood in the clump of trees, the first yellow aspen leaves lying on the sod roof around the smoke vent. The men following him would surely completely destroy the settlement this time when they couldn't find him there. And later, anyone spotting him in the forest would hurry off toward town with the news and they would take up the hunt again. It would probably be just as well to flee north with his wife and daughter the same day.

The millstone was standing where it had always stood with a little rainwater in it. It would be handy to have but was too heavy to carry. He could probably manage to grind a new one once they got to a safe place. And it would be a while before he could exchange goods for grain to mill anyway.

He picked up some other things he found too – a small sledge-hammer with a broken handle, a rusty spindle-whorl, a little pot with a handle for hanging above the fire, a couple of whetstones. The sun was hanging above the cove, and the trees were glimmering yellow and red. It was all so calm and peaceful – maybe they could stay in the cave until the worst was over. During the winter they would at least be left in peace, although their footprints in the fresh snow could be dangerous.

Relieved, Holme headed back toward the cave. He never retraced his own steps, so as not to wear a path through the grass. When he looked back, the field rat was still scampering among the yellow stubble and the chirping sparrows were fluttering from sheaf to sheaf. The mist, gliding now in light veils across the surface of the water, would soon completely dissipate in the sun. Holme sensed somehow that he had known all this from the beginning of time. He wasn't sure just how old he was, but Ausi had notched a short piece of wood every summer since Tora was born.

He walked back through the still and somewhat pungent autumn forest. Gorgeous mushrooms were glowing, leaves constantly falling. Near his path grew a number of hazel trees, and he walked over to see if the nuts were ready. A young bird flew off with a shriek from under the bushes suffused with sunlight.

The nuts were brown and lying on the ground. He picked up a few and put them into the iron pot. Tora would be glad, of course. If they didn't have to run, they could come back and gather a big store for the winter.

In town the chieftain's wife, Svein's mother, fought bitterly for what she thought were her rights. After the town's Christian chieftain had tired of her complaint and had driven her away, she managed to get permission to meet the king at his farmstead a couple of hours away by boat.[1]

Blight had not touched the king's crop, perhaps because he was living on an island, but he construed it as a blessing from the gods. And so he was cheerful when the middle-aged woman with the hard face came seeking justice from him. Svein walked behind her, and the thrall they had paid to do the rowing stayed behind in the boat. He looked with curiosity and admiration at the king's dragon ship lying outside the blockade.

Against the wall of the main building stood some chairs in the sunshine, and the king invited the woman and her son to join him

1. Fridegård never mentions the name of this market-town, but it is unmistakably Birka, a major Viking trade center that was established around 800 A.D. and flourished for about two hundred years. Its ruins lie about twenty miles west of present-day Stockholm. Fridegård uses the town as the setting for most of his Holme trilogy.

Throughout the trilogy about Holme, Fridegård relies on archeological evidence, cultural studies, and a saint's life to substantiate his description of the period and give his work verisimilitude (see the following notes and the afterword to *Land of Wooden Gods*). In this final volume of the trilogy, he continues to rely for the outlines of the historical narrative on Bishop Rimbert's ninth-century life of Saint Ansgar, the German monk who undertook the first recorded mission to Sweden in ca. 830. The work is entitled *Vita Anskarii* in the Latin and has been translated into English as *Anskar: Apostle of the North, 801–865* by there. He listened quietly to the woman's long history of suffering. As she spoke, one of his most trusted men came and stood by in silence. When the woman began telling about Holme's throwing a rock that injured her son, she got up and showed the king her angry and glaring son's stiff neck.

The king was perfectly familiar with Holme's history in town, so he was more interested in hearing about his past life as a slave. He thought briefly of the Danish king's advice to make a man like Holme his friend and warrior, but he knew he couldn't. His men would never acknowledge him as their equal, and strife and discontent would follow. They would withdraw from Holme, not because he had committed a crime, but because he had been a thrall. The town merchants were different; they had accepted him because of his skill and strength, but the warriors had always kept their distance.

The woman finished her tale of woe by demanding her rights. Holme should be put to death and his wife and daughter returned to her. She should have help, too, with rebuilding the old settlement – Svein, soon grown, would need a farmstead like his father's. That one was in a good place and produced good harvests.

Charles H. Robinson (London: The Society for the Propagation of the Gospel in Foreign Parts, 1921). Fridegård is not as heavily dependent on Rimbert in *Sacrificial Smoke* as he is in volumes one and two of the trilogy, however. It seems, for example, that he still intends the chieftain in *Sacrificial Smoke* to be the chieftain from the previous volume, although that chieftain was modeled on a man named Herigar who died in 851, a couple of years before the events described here. Fridegård likewise does not seem to relinquish Björn, a king mentioned in Rimbert and depicted in *People of the Dawn*, although Olaf, perhaps Björn's son, replaced Björn by about 853—before the events of *Sacrificial Smoke*. Fridegård increases the ambiguity about the kings by mentioning the two of them toward the end of *Sacrificial Smoke*, but the whole problem may ultimately derive from Rimbert, who also introduces the second king in chapter 26 without having explained what happened to the first. For a detailed chronology based on Rimbert, see note 6, p. 61.

In addition, she would need three or four men and a couple of women thralls.

The king replied that he had already sent out a number of riders that very day to capture Holme. They were under strict orders to capture and kill him and then bring his body to town. She wasn't the only one who wanted some peace. He also agreed that she should get Holme's wife and daughter back since they were only runaway thralls. But she would have to get any other thralls she needed on her own. There had to be a number of them wandering around who'd be willing to follow her to the settlement.

After some food and drink, the mother and son returned to their boat where the thrall was asleep on the seat. The woman, feeling satisfied with what she had gained, scolded him sternly. It was just a matter of time now before she could gaze on Holme's corpse and reclaim his wife and daughter. Finally, after all these years, she would be happy. She sat in the boat enjoying the thought of what she was going to do to them. And she fantasized about building the family settlement bigger and more beautiful than ever. She and Svein would be in command, and everything would be like it was in bygone, happier days.

A little shadow now and then clouded her dreams. The chieftain had called her "heathen" when he drove her out of town. Many of the most important people there – both men and women – had been baptized. Maybe in the long run only the people of lowest rank and the slaves would stick to the ancient wooden gods. She didn't want to be one of them; her husband had been a great chieftain. Maybe she should accept baptism, and then the chieftain and many others would be on her side. Besides, for all she knew, Christ just might be the most powerful of the gods.

She tried to discuss the future with Svein, but he either answered curtly or not at all as he gazed out over the water. He only really listened when she talked about the search for Holme that now was in full swing. Sacrifices to the gods had already begun over this matter, but now she didn't exactly know what she wanted. Once ashore, they walked across the field separating the Christian church from the heathen temple, and she looked from side to side, not knowing who could bring success to the warriors hunting Holme. She turned finally to Christ. If any of these gods were protecting Holme, it would have to be one of the ancient wooden ones.

The church was empty and she walked all the way up to the altar in her curiosity. A gold and red picture was hanging there, brought by the Christians from their homeland. A cloth with some beautiful vessels on it was lying on the altar.

She looked around for a priest to talk with. Svein yelled something to her through the open door and kept going. She could hear various sounds from the heathen temple, including the regular bleating of a sheep or a goat that would surely be sacrificed. The woman wondered what she could offer Christ to make Him take her side against Holme. Maybe just a promise. Then if Christ failed, she wouldn't have to keep it.

Something was moving in the little room behind the altar, and a man soon emerged. After hearing the woman's story, he told her that there were no priests in town but one or two were on their way. In the meantime, the chieftain was leading the church services. The man was positive Christ would help her if she made a donation to the church. He'd also heard that the new priests would erect a bigger church – one bigger and taller than the heathen temple. Two bells would ring out from it and render the wooden gods powerless.

And as she glanced furtively out the door toward the hall of the wooden gods, the woman promised Christ a gift for the new church. In exchange He should arrange for Holme to die and his wife and daughter to be returned to her, just like the king had promised.

But she kept wondering how that tiny picture with the drooping head could be stronger than the ancient and stern wooden gods. She'd wait and see, though. Once He had fulfilled his part of the bargain, the gift would be on its way.

She passed between both temples again as she departed, again feeling great distrust for Christ. His temple was desolate and empty except when the Christians gathered and sang their tedious songs. But the heathen temple was always bustling and full of laughter. It would smell of roasted meat and the offerings of beer would sizzle on the hot stones. The rejuvenated settlement would seem bleak without a little heathen shrine and a god in it looking out over the fields. You could make sacrifices to him at various times and keep yourself happy all the while with food and drink. So had her forefathers done from time immemorial.

But she could still do what many others had – cling to Christ sometimes without relinquishing the ancient gods. It would all depend on who gave her the most help during the next few days.

It was a group of sullen, tired warriors who, on the king's orders, armed themselves again to hunt Holme through the mainland forests. They mumbled in their beards that they had taken him back to town once already but someone had let him escape. They weren't going to spend their whole lives searching for some thrall in the woods, no matter how criminal and dangerous he might be. Their duty was to defend the town.

Their anger erupted when they gathered around the chieftain. Angry words were flying from every direction, and the warriors insisted again that they should be fighting for their king, not forever engaging in this manhunt.

"Let the thrall go," a voice called out and several other voices rose in agreement. Though too proud to admit it, the men knew that some of them would never come back alive if they ever caught Holme. But if they left him alone, they'd probably seen the last of him on the island. Why hunt him?

The chieftain concurred but he had his orders. He tried reasoning with the warriors again, this time threatening them with the king's wrath. But they laughed scornfully and repeated that they were warriors, not thrall overseers. Some said that if the gods really wanted Holme dead, he wouldn't have gotten away so many times.

With that the chieftain's ears perked up and he saw a possible way out. They'd cast lots to see if the gods wanted them to keep hunting Holme. If the lot went against him, the warriors would abide by it. If not, the king would retract his order and not thwart the will of the gods.

He surveyed the warriors again before making his suggestion, and he could see that his hesitation had helped increase their resolve. Nothing but the will of the gods could get them into the forest now.

A little while later, they were all gathered at the place of council outside town, their horses wandering loose and snorting among the burial mounds a short distance away. Children, women, merchants, craftsmen – everyone had come to see what was going on. Svein and his mother had come too, and her face contorted with anger when she heard why they were casting lots. She sensed that most of them would just as soon let Holme go. But she and her son would never have a day's rest as long as he was alive and free.

She saw one of the heathen priests cutting twigs off the apple tree standing nearby, small red fruit glistening among the yellow foliage. He put a different mark on each twig, and the chieftain stood there examining the marks one after another. The warriors' faces had grown yet more sullen and angry; they knew they'd have to bow to the will of the gods, regardless of how the lot fell.

The priests spread a large, pastel yellow cloth on the ground and secured the corners with stones so the wind wouldn't catch them. Tiny black autumn flies immediately lit on the cloth, and a spider numb from the frost crept slowly across one of the corners. The temple attendants emerged from the temple carrying an image of a god between them. They set it down next to the cloth. An unpleasant smell of stale blood wafted on the wind from it. The warriors and other people looked at it with respect, but the Christian chieftain turned away in displeasure and disgust. He would rather have washed his hands of all this.

A whisper passed through the crowd when everything was ready, and then there was complete silence. A gust of wind urged the yellow leaves still on the tree into a rustling dance, then died away as a stillness settled over everything in the clear autumn day.

Everyone took the stillness as a sign, so the priest cast the twigs down on the cloth. When they came to rest, he got on his knees to decipher the will of the gods. The warriors were mistrustful and huddled around him to see for themselves. They depended on no one, neither the priest nor the chieftain, because they had been deceived too many times before. The chieftain was standing up behind them in disdain.

The priest loudly counted the twigs, and when he was done it had all turned out as the warriors had hoped. They should not hunt the thrall, but should stay home instead. The priest interpreted the sign and said that an enemy fleet lying in wait would have attacked if the warriors had left the town defenseless. Now they wouldn't dare.

The warriors rose in satisfaction, looking triumphantly at their chieftain. But he was just as glad as they were although he didn't show it. He would much rather stay in town because he was expecting a ship from the Christian lands, and he too had had his fill of Holme. Besides, he knew that most of his people would follow what they believed was the will of the gods even in this case.

But there was one observer who would not tolerate the outcome. Svein's mother had followed the casting of lots with mounting anxiety and rage. When the satisfied warriors started back to the fortress, she began hurling insults at them in her shrill voice. They were lazy and had cowered before a single thrall. Then she turned on the chieftain and threatened him with the king's ire. She had talked with him the same day and he had promised that a company of warriors would hunt Holme down and bring his body back to town. And his family would be returned to their rightful owner.

The men listened to her but didn't bother to respond. They looked the other way and talked softly among themselves while they gathered their horses and walked toward the fortress. Then the chieftain ordered his thralls to man one of the smaller boats, probably so he could report to the king.

The council place was soon empty. The gods were put back in place and the cloth was removed. The apple-tree twigs, perhaps having saved Holme's life, were lying discarded in the grass. You could still hear the woman's distant angry yelping as she and her son retreated to their home at the far end of town.

Holme stuck to the ridge all day so he could keep an eye on the dried marshland dotted by the dwarf pines growing on tall lingonberry tufts. His enemies would have to show up there or in the dense woods on the opposite slope. The ridge was too bumpy and rocky for their horses.

15

Ausi and Tora were trying to make the cave more comfortable for the next night. They were chattering away like a couple of young girls, seemingly unaware of the danger threatening them. The cave's mossy ceiling was covered with dark red clumps of lingonberries, and Tora would occasionally grab a handful and stuff them into her mouth.

Holme, his mind still not made up, paced heavily back and forth on the ridge, anxious as a bear. It was so peaceful up there that it was hard to grasp the immensity of the danger. But his enemies would probably gallop in every direction through the forest that day. Not alone – they wouldn't dare – but in groups, and if they discovered the cave while he, Ausi, and Tora were inside, that would be the end of them all.

Holme was also thinking that they ought to have some meat or fish. The bread that Ausi had baked on the hot stone early in the morning would get tiresome. He might still have time, and there ought to be a domestic pig or two still at the settlement. He should have thought of that when he was there at sunrise. It hadn't been too many days before when he had seen two of them looking down on the settlement from the edge of the forest. They were already half wild so they spooked suddenly and disappeared in a waddling gallop through the underbrush.

A smiling mother and daughter greeted him when he walked back to the cave. They hadn't worried too much about his deciding to return to the settlement – they knew he was better off alone than when he had them or others to look after. They had promised to keep hidden and to be on the lookout while he was away.

For the second time that day Holme was looking at the settlement, but this time it was more dangerous. He turned an ear toward the forest, but all was quiet. A noise now and then from the lake made his face tense for a moment. A pig's muffled grunting came from an alder grove to the left of the jetty.

He listened again before venturing down the slope. If his enemies showed up, he could probably hide in the grove and then slip off into the forest farther away along the shore. The ridge near the cave branched down to the cove farther off, and he could make it home that way in just about any degree of darkness.

A lot depended on how wild the pig had become. Holme should have taken his bow with him, but he had always relied more on his ax and knife. The pig was probably still a little tame since it had stuck so close to the settlement.

The grunting stopped while he was still a ways from the grove, and he knew he'd been discovered. As softly as he had walked, the pig had still picked up his steps in its funnel-like ears. But he knew pigs well; instead of trying to slip away, it would stand stock-still until he was right next to it.

Holme carefully parted the alder bushes, then stepped into the darkness that smelled of mire. Right in front of him were some fresh tracks with yellow leaves trampled down into them. He stood still, letting his eyes grow accustomed to the dark inside. A few treetops rose high above the grove, and the leaves still clinging to them glowed a gaudy yellow in the afternoon sun.

It took a while before anything happened. He had begun to fear he hadn't really heard anything, but the tracks didn't lie. A single fly was buzzing somewhere outside the foliage where the sun was shining. Just as Holme was about to take a few steps forward, the white of an eye flashed and the pig's gray silhouette soon appeared against the thicket and mud.

But then came the hard part. If the half-wild pig ran away, Holme wouldn't be able to catch it, and he wasn't close enough yet to use his ax. For a moment he thought about throwing the ax, but the chances of his hitting the pig hard enough to penetrate it were slight. Besides, the pig would probably take off as soon as he raised his weapon.

Holme had always had more of a way with animals than with people, and it struck him that he might be able to calm the pig. He began talking gently to it and saw the eye flash again. But the pig stayed completely still, and Holme carefully moved one foot forward. If he could get three or four steps closer, he could dive on the pig, which was only half grown. It had to be one born during the spring and so must have seen people the entire summer.

Holme took another step and nothing happened. He kept talking calmly, receiving at least one weak grunt in response. That gave him confidence and he kept moving forward. When he was only four or five steps away, the pig started backing away, grunting, blinking, sniffing, and stretching its snout toward him. For a moment, he felt compassion for it and considered sparing its life. Pigs were somehow the animals of thralls, kindred spirits.

Many years before, he had maliciously and gleefully plunged his knife into one of the master's young pigs in the forest swamp while the swineherds napped. He had just needed food for his wife and child then too, but he hadn't felt what he did now. Since that time he had tasted freedom, and the pig before him now resembled himself – free but pursued.

The pig, friendly and curious, kept moving out of his way, grunting. Suddenly it came out through the farthest thicket, and the sun shone on its bristly back, caked with dried mud. In the same instant, it let go a terrified, indistinct scolding sound and rushed away. But Holme was tight on its heels, blocking its retreat into the grove.

The pig dashed back and forth on the few feet of shoreline, Holme between it and safety. Holme's compassion was gone now.

He concentrated only on the blow he had to strike. But landing it wasn't easy, and he twice struck only the air. When the pig could find no way back into the grove, it ran into a space under the logs and stones. It got stuck in there, and Holme managed to grab a hind leg. The pig had time to let out a few long cries of distress before Holme pulled it out and stunned it with the butt of the ax.

Holme got up looking tensely toward the edge of the forest by the settlement, but there was nothing there and he heard no riders. The pig was still kicking in the gravel, so he stabbed it in the throat and lifted it into the air until all the blood drained out. Then he rinsed it clean by the shore. For a moment the water among the stones turned pink, but more waves rolled in, washing away every trace.

Holme carried the carcass to the grove so he couldn't be seen from the settlement. There he chopped a strong stick, slit the pig's hind legs with his knife, then shoved the stick under the tendons to make it easier to carry the load. The sun would set soon, and it was time to return to the cave. He had long had a store of salt there for preserving meat.

He had forgotten his pursuers for a while but on the way back it struck him again what danger he was in. The first day was almost over and nothing had happened, but that didn't mean he could feel safe. Besides, he didn't know what was happening at the cave, a thought that made him quicken his pace. He passed the old master's burial mound where two small aspen trees had started growing on the south side. They had already lost all their leaves, which now lay like a yellow rug around their feet. Many years had passed since the chieftain's bones and ashes had been laid in the mound, and many things had happened at his settlement.

Holme knew he had to reach a decision. He could flee into the unknown with its dangers and hardships or stay here, forever sneaking around like a night animal. He had no other choice. Or did he? A thought came like a flash, stopping him dead in his tracks. Then he shook his head and walked on.

But the thought stuck with him, whispering in his ear. He had seen the king on more than one occasion, and there was something about him he liked. His simple clothes, his grave, friendly look. Rumor had it that he treated his thralls well. He might understand. But Holme had to talk with him alone. That was impossible in town, but maybe at his farmstead, a long boat ride away. Holme knew he'd try anyway before disappearing into the forests forever. As long as nothing had happened at the cave, that is.

He walked faster as he got closer, the pig swinging from his shoulder. But all was quiet, the sun was down, and the grass was stiffening again with the frost. The hunt probably wouldn't begin before the next day.

Mother and daughter crawled happily out of the cave and caressed him lovingly until his eyes took on a friendly luster. They were delighted with the meat and praised him for his hunting. Now they dared build a fire to cook the meat together with some broth and roots, and Holme quickly constructed a tripod for suspending the pot over the fire. The three of them were soon hungrily eating the meal, their eyes and teeth glistening. Mother and daughter, enjoying the moment, had no fears. They had food, a roof over their heads, and protection.

Holme, however, was thinking that weathering a winter in the cave would be hard even without pursuers. He had heard of people long ago living in caves all year round, but the winters were probably milder then, and people were used to cold and hunger. It wouldn't be easy to get food when the snow was deep in the forest and thick ice covered the lakes. He had to do something and quickly. But not tomorrow; maybe the day after. If his pursuers hadn't come by then, something had probably happened in town. He thought that foreign vessels might have sailed in, friendly or hostile, and he had to find out. Not knowing was worse than anything else because he could never feel at ease about his wife and daughter in the cave, could never go far without stopping and listening. Things just couldn't go on that way.

At midnight Holme left the cave, followed by Ausi's anxious warnings. Tora was confident as usual; she always thought there wasn't a man alive who could get the better of her father.

Holme walked for hours while the autumn moon sank toward the forest's crest. He wanted to reach a spot just about directly opposite the king's farmstead, so he wouldn't have far to row. He had always felt more comfortable in the woods than on the open lake.

The night forest was alive everywhere he walked, and he kept his ax constantly ready. Wolves and wild boars didn't concern him much, but the invisible, evil powers you can't defend yourself against did. The older Holme grew the more he believed in them, and he was certain that all the magicians in the area were hard at work casting spells in his path. When he heard the sound of paws moving softly in the moss, when he saw a pair of cold, green eyes glowing through a thicket, or when an owl let out a shrill hoot, he couldn't stop the chill running up and down his spine. This had never happened to him before, and he wished he was in a fury or a bad mood. Then no kind of danger frightened him, neither visible nor invisible.

Much of this probably also had to do with the mission he was on. He was an outlaw and anyone at all had the right to kill him. And now he was on his way to visit the king who had given that order. Nothing like this had ever happened before, so this journey might be his last. But he had had to do something, and the danger he faced would be equally great no matter what. With wife and daughter, he couldn't live the life of an outlaw this close to town. If his talk with the king did no good, he'd return to the cave, and then it would be time to leave.

Holme finally happened upon a scarcely noticeable path and followed it to the shore. Walking was easier here, although the occasional boulder jutting into the water forced him back into the forest. He saw a boat by a little jetty and moved closer for a better look. It wasn't well secured, so he probably could have gotten it loose, but the farmstead was still too far away. Then he saw a sharply pitched roof outlined against the blue-green night sky and walked closer. Everything was quiet, but a trace of smoke was still rising, shadowlike, from the smoke vent, and the withered grass at the peak of the sod roof whispered in the night wind.

The moon was sinking fast, growing larger and redder as it neared the treetops. Once it disappeared, the night would be dark for a good while, making it more difficult for him to find his way in the forest and bogs. Sometimes the forest reached all the way to the water, its huge trees leaning hesitantly over it. In a couple of places forest streams rippled past, and several times cold water seeped through his goatskin shoes as he hopped the streams or slogged through their sedge-covered banks.

The shore soon became more even and he could move faster. Then it changed direction and the moon wandered from woods to lake. An endless red stream shot across the water, broken here and there by dark flecks that were probably belts of reeds. He'd be directly opposite the king's farmstead soon. He knew some fishermen lived in the area, and he'd borrow a boat from them.

Several boats of various sizes lay at the shore, but the fishing village was still asleep. Holme walked down to a jetty where two boats were tied and stepped into the smaller one. He figured the fisherman could get along with one until he returned. It wouldn't take long. He'd either have to flee or reach an agreement with the king and would have to return this way in either case.

The thin layer of ice that forms at night clanged against the side of the boat as it cut a furrow into the high reeds. The seabirds, chattering in astonishment, raced farther back into the reeds. Massive and red now, the moon finally sank in the endless distance, and Holme somehow felt more alone after it was gone. It had followed him all night long. For a long time afterward, the horizon stayed a shimmering red where it had sunk.

The boat creaked with every tug of the oars, but it didn't matter. No one would be waiting for him. They wouldn't dream he'd come this way, much less try to find the king. He didn't even know himself why he was doing this. He knew what might happen, but he was tired of hiding in a hole like a wolf or fox.

The king's forest was soon before him and Holme rowed cautiously to land. He had guessed the time right; the sun was just beginning to rise, and now he'd have time to search the surrounding area before anyone woke up. He had to know the best escape route into the forest in case he needed it. He had decided not to fight the king's men if he could avoid it. It was enough that the whole town was after him.

In the distance far across the water he could barely make out the island where the town was and wondered if he'd ever return. Then he hid the boat in the bushes by the shore and walked toward the king's farmstead.

At the King's farmstead, they had already started brewing the beer that was to last the whole winter. Everyone was in a congenial mood after a good harvest of barley and hops. With his own hands the king laid crossed sticks of mountain ash in the brewing vats, and placed a flint ax in the vat of brewer's malt. He and his people believed that the ax, a bolt from the thunder god, would protect the malt. If you didn't have a thunderbolt you'd put a silver object of some kind into the vat or you could almost be sure that magic would destroy the brew.

When the beer was ready and tasted it would be left standing until the midwinter sacrifice. Then everybody, both people and animals, got their share. The king himself would soak a piece of bread in the beer and give it to his horses and cows. They would snort and sniff at it a while but soon begin to eat it. When it was gone, they would lick their chops and whinny and moo wildly for more, and that was a good sign for the coming year.

When the morning light shone through the openings in the building where the king was brewing his beer, it fell on what looked very much like a troll. For many generations it had been the custom that the ugliest man around would brew the beer to insure success. If it wouldn't ferment, you could see him running around the brewing chamber, yelling and conjuring wildly. The whole time he would pull his hair or beat himself with his fists. If nothing else helped, he would calm down, fetch a big piece of meat, and lay it under the brewing vat. But he didn't often have to resort to making that sacrifice to a minor deity. They did only what their fathers had taught them.[2]

Holme sneaked up to the sleeping farmstead. It was still early so he wasn't afraid of being discovered. And if a sleepy thrall on his way to work in the king's barn should discover him in the gray dawn, he'd only hurry inside faster, thinking he had just seen a

---

2. Ebbe Schön, *Jan Fridegård och forntiden. En studie i diktverk och källor* (Uppsala: Almqvist & Wiksell, 1973), pp. 111–12, shows that the details about beer and beer brewing come from Hilding Celander's book about the pagan Nordic yule: *Nordisk jul, I. Julen i gammaldags bondesed* (Stockholm, 1928).

troll or maybe the spirit of one of the king's relatives. He had shown himself a few times before as a portent that something was going to happen.

But there was no movement at the farmstead, no dogs barking. Holme admired the large, well-built buildings and walked closer. The hinges on the doors were shaped like dragon heads, and he became curious. He touched them, following the curves with his fingers, and then remembered: he had forged these very hinges himself. He also remembered when the farmstead's foreman had brought that assignment to the smithy.

He still didn't know how he could arrange to talk with the king, but he depended on that power in his life that had always made things happen just at the right moment. It was either good or bad, and it wasn't easy to tell. Sometimes what he thought was bad turned out to be good in the end and sometimes just the opposite. He would stick close to the farmstead and wait for something to happen.

It was growing light quickly, so Holme walked back to the edge of the forest. He would hide there until the people were up. It would be obvious soon if the king was there.

He hadn't seen the king's harbor on the way over; a point of land had blocked it from view. It occurred to Holme to see if the ships were there or not. The king had two ships with dragon heads and many smaller boats as well.

He sneaked around the farmstead and moved toward the lake. The first thing he saw was a man on a hill, looking across the water. He was probably the harbor guard, there both day and night. There was a birch-bark box next to the man, probably for his food. Holme felt hungry when he saw it, but he had some bread and lean pork on him. He'd find a safe place to eat soon.

He couldn't get any closer to the lake without the guard seeing him, but beyond the bushes he stood behind he could see two golden dragon heads sticking up, red mouths gaping toward land. The king had to be at his farmstead. Numerous rows of poles for drying the fishing nets stood by the harbor, and the sound of cawing crows and shrieking seagulls wafted by Holme from that direction. The cool breeze coming from lake and harbor carried the smell of water and raw fish.

The guard yawned with a howl that sounded eerie through the silence, and then he looked around. When he turned to the lake again, Holme went back to the forest beyond the farmstead. He sat down on a low rock at the edge of the forest so he could keep an eye on the farmstead, and then he took out his food.

His thoughts carried him to his wife and daughter as he ate the bread and meat. As he had done many times before, he wondered now what would happen to them if he were gone. Deep inside he knew: a thrall's despicable life with all the drudgery, the beatings, the tongue lashings, the rapes, and the babies left to die in the forest. Ausi and Tora would be treated even more cruelly because they had been his wife and daughter. And Tora would get the brunt of it; like him she would never bend, never give in. She would fight back as he had done. She was a girl and weak but she would still fight. Holme knew he had to live for their sake.

He sat and watched the sun come up. It flashed among the trees, and the stubble fields between the farmstead and the forest turned a sudden yellow and took on a warmer look than they had before. The rich, black earth beneath the stubble began to steam.

The farmstead was waking up and starting its day. Someone who must have been the king's foreman walked around putting all the thralls to work. Animal tenders were already at it, and from where he sat Holme could see a couple of women thralls carrying their milk pails from the barn. Smoke rose straight up through the smoke vent, and animals were mooing, neighing, grunting, and barking at the brand-new day.

Holme felt once more a deep yearning for that life, for that peace and that work. Why weren't they possible for everyone? Why did he have to be hunted like an animal when all he wanted to do was work and live in peace with everyone? Defending your farmstead or village against invaders – that had to be done, but why did men fight and hunt each other?

His thoughts began to settle on the freedom that everyone ought to have, but he didn't let them stay there. Many strong, good men lay slaughtered and buried like animals, just because they had dared think of that freedom and had tried to attain it. That was why Holme was being hunted and had to flee from everything worth living for.

Even more powerfully than before, it struck him again how dangerous and hopeless the day ahead of him was. If he did get to talk to the king, he still wouldn't gain anything. It wasn't easy for him to talk, and the king probably wouldn't understand him, understand that he had never harmed any human being if he could have avoided it, and that all thralls were like him in this regard. Well, maybe not all; there were some who were cowardly, who would betray their friends just to get in good with their masters. On the other hand, there were plenty of bad, merciless masters, too.

But here he was. He had traveled a long way and wouldn't turn back without completing his mission. The king would probably soon make himself seen at his farmstead.

The sun shone through the windows and struck against the far wall. Various wall decorations, tapestries, and weapons hung in the crystal-clear light. When the king awoke, the wall caught his eye, and he felt happy and at ease. Everything he had touched this autumn had been successful. Before returning to their land, the Christian priests had told him that he had Christ to thank for it all, and perhaps that was true. In any case, he had promised that the Christians in town would be free to hold services even without a priest. It was only about a fourth of the town's population that was in question, and when things went against them many would turn back to the old gods.

New priests were coming in the spring. They had been coming and going for years; not one of them had the courage to stay. Their lives were in constant danger, the old gods still lived a vigorous life, and the Christian priests had to walk in and out of the church constantly surrounded by sacrificial smoke. They were the ones, though, who had chosen to build their church as close to the heathen temple as possible so they could defy the wooden gods. So the Christian bells had rung out over the water for many years, but to little avail. On calm, clear days you could hear the bells all the way to the king's farmstead.

The king heard his men talking out in the hall. They were probably starting to get up and inspect their weapons. The beer would be ready that morning. Everything had gone well so the ugly brewmaster would get a princely reward. He had managed to hold all evil away from the brew, and the beer ought to have settled overnight.

The king thought too about their casting lots soon to see if the gods would give them good fortune for a spring expedition. They were running low on a number of items in town and the surrounding countryside. There wasn't enough silver but they could get some by laying seige to a town and making it pay a ransom. They could put to sea well before the new priests came with their dour faces and punishing words. On such a journey everyone had to be happy and filled with hope.

The king got up and straightened his clothes as pleasant thoughts kept buzzing in his head. Before he went out he combed his hair and beard and put on a gold-embroidered cap. His men were up and busy in the outer room and hall, and a couple of them already sat with their bearded heads bent over the chessboard. A couple of costly objects stood shining on a shelf in the morning sunlight, and everyone passing by had to glance at them. They were a couple of multicolored Roman glasses, and there weren't many of such things in the entire country.[3]

Out in the brewery, the ugly brewmaster was watching over his work when the king came in. He sprang to his feet, an expression of either anxiety or pride on his face. He had managed to protect the beer from evil powers but it had taken its toll on him. Now all was well, the danger almost past.

After saying a few words to him, the king took a ladle of beer, pushed his beard aside, and drank, yellow pearls rolling down onto his clothes. The beer was still too fresh to drink and he quickly put down the ladle. But he smiled with satisfaction and the brewmaster's ugly face lit up. The king ordered that his men should each have a tankard of the new beer for their morning meal. Then it would be left untouched until the winter sacrifice.

When he came out of the brewery, he didn't feel like returning to his house. Outside, there was a nice balance of warmth from the rising sun and chill from the remaining frost. He stopped for a while in the warmth by the log wall. Then he walked toward the outlying buildings where it smelled of mire and excrement when

3. Although there is some evidence of glassmaking in Scandinavia during this period, fine glass was imported for the wealthy. See James Graham-Campbell, *The Viking World* (New Haven: Ticknor & Fields, 1980), pp. 88–91.

the sun shone. All that was missing were the swarms of buzzing summer flies, and he thought about that a moment.

Everything was as it should be in the outlying buildings, so he was soon outside again. He somehow felt better than he had for a long time. Everything was calm and easy that morning. The harvested barley field lay before him, and he walked out into it. There was a lot of grain left among the stalks, and he would tell the women thralls to pick it when they got the chance. He kept ambling across the field, picking up a stone now and then and tossing it into one of the little furrows that striped the field. Someone had left a sickle on a big rock overnight and now it had red rust stains. Picking it up, the king muttered to himself that the guilty party was going to hear about this.

At the edge of the forest stood some aspen trees with smooth, grayish-green trunks and carpets of yellow leaves lying at their feet. The air smelled fresh but a little pungent. The king was feeling even better, but it didn't occur to him that the stong beer might have gone to his head. Since he hadn't eaten anything, he tolerated less alcohol than usual.

He kept walking deeper into the forest, looking around. He saw a couple of spruce trees with dried-out trunks that would have to be felled for firewood. One had a hole in it and a beautiful bird popped out and flashed its head to both sides before catapulting into the air and flying away with a series of shrill cries.

The king walked a few steps further without noticing that a massive figure slowly, quietly stole behind the trees and bushes in a semicircle around him. The figure had been sitting on a rock and had seen the king crossing the fields. He had slipped away but was now back on the rock, which lay between the king and his farmstead.

The king looked at him in surprise, and it took a moment before the contented expression in his eyes disappeared. At first, he couldn't believe the smith was sitting there on the rock. The thrall couldn't have come to the farmstead without someone seeing him and sounding the alarm. But when the king remembered everything he had heard about Holme, it didn't seem unlikely that he had once again fooled everyone who was after him. But what was he doing here?

The king's and thrall's eyes met, and the feeling of terror that had already gripped the king died away. The thrall wasn't after his life – he could see that in his eyes. They were on guard and sad at one and the same time. The king took in the entire figure before him and began to understand the saga of this thrall better. There was something about him that commanded your attention. You couldn't just disdainfully walk by.

The thrall didn't move and the king sensed he was waiting for something. It was difficult to feel like a king out here; in the forest it was man against man.

'You're Holme,' he said, and the figure made an affirmative gesture.

'What do you want here?'

Then the thrall began talking in his deep, gruff voice. He wasn't accustomed to talking and soon fell silent, frustrated at not being able to find the right words. The king began to think that all this was an exciting adventure. He thought again about what the Danish king had said – he had to make such a man his friend. Everyone knew what having him as an enemy meant.

The king's good mood completely revived, and he jokingly asked when it had become the custom for a king to stand and his subject to sit. Holme understood immediately and stood up. He took his ax from its leather case, and the king's face grew tense with fear. But Holme put the long-handled ax against the trunk of an aspen tree, as the king marveled over this thrall who comported himself like a chieftain. Holme did not want to take unfair advantage of an unarmed king.

The rock had enough room for two, and the king gestured for Holme to sit beside him. He could soon tell that Holme had difficulty expressing himself, so he started asking him questions. That worked better, and the king, who was a good judge of people, could soon tell that Holme was speaking the truth.

They sat on the rock for a long time; a woman's bright voice called the king's name twice from the farmstead, but he just smiled and ignored it. To his surprise, he began to understand that the thrall smith, considered the greatest evildoer in the kingdom, had had no choice but to do what he had done. The king would have done the same thing himself. Strange sensations were stirring deep in the king's heart. He considered himself a fair ruler, but the smith's story made him uncomfortable. He had never known or understood that a thrall could have so much substance.

But he didn't dare try to understand the thralls' battle for freedom. What would happen to order in the land if there were no thralls? Who would work the fields, care for the animals, build boats, and erect buildings? The farmsteads would fall to ruin, and the harvests would be destroyed when the masters went on a raid or were themselves besieged.

The king pushed those thoughts away until later. Right now, he had to do something about the man sitting next to him. He had no desire to send Holme out to be killed, but his warriors would never take him into their company. There had to be another way.

The woman's voice called anxiously a third time, and there was a group of men gathered at the farmstead, obviously ready to search for the king. He got up and told Holme to follow him. He waited while Holme got his ax, then walked in front of him. Something told the king that he didn't have to fear this massive, dangerous man walking behind him, carrying a huge ax. The king felt proud and happy to think that he, alone and unarmed, was leading in the man whom it would normally take several armed men to overcome.

The queen and a group of warriors, the foreman in front, awaited them at the farmstead. The queen's lips turned white and a number of warriors grabbed their weapons, but the king waved them off. As he drew closer, he told them that Holme had come seeking protection and justice and that no harm should come to him before his case had been tried. Until then he would stay at the farmstead and no one was to bother him. As everyone knew, he could defend himself. No one had to fear him either; he never attacked unprovoked, only defended himself and his family.

When Holme had heard the king's words, he put his ax aside again, and the king smiled at his warriors in smug satisfaction. He had tamed the wild beast his way. Now everyone was curious about Holme, whom they had heard so much about. The warriors looked with reluctant admiration at the well-built body; the thralls, at a distance, looked at him with secret pride because he was one of them. The queen, who had trembled when she saw such a powerful, ominous figure with a glistening ax behind the king, looked at him now with something like gratitude. She knew that no one could have saved the king's life had Holme chosen to kill him.

The morning meal had long been ready and set out, so the queen gave the signal to go to the long tables. The brewmaster had carried out the king's order, and a few women thralls brought beer tankards from the brewery. Holme got to sit at the end of the warriors' table and he too received a foaming tankard of beer. The rumor about who he was had already spread, and the women thralls kept turning toward him in curiosity as they walked around serving the men.

Meanwhile, the king told his men what he thought of the

smith's story. He told them about Holme's constantly being pursued, about his once being the master smith in town. When he said that, several heads turned to look at Holme and then back again to look meaningfully at each other. Many of them were still proudly carrying weapons of his making.

The king avoided talking about the thralls' battle for freedom, which had cost so many lives. But he did say that the Danish king had advised him to make Holme one of his warriors. He saw his men stiffen in pride and arrogance and knew they would never accept the smith as their equal. And so people from town would demand Holme's surrender as soon as it became known he was at the king's farmstead.

As he pondered, the king heard a warrior tell another in a low voice the Holme had done the metalwork for the king's farmstead. He hadn't been aware of that; his foreman took care of such matters. But it gave him an idea. Holme could be the smith on the farmstead and his story would finally fall into oblivion. He would just have to stay away from town for the first few years.

The king was happy with that solution. He didn't want to let the man most people hated or feared out of his sight. A thrall had never before become so renowned, the subject of so much conversation. When foreign kings or chieftains came, they would get to hear his saga and perhaps see some proof of his powers.

The warriors sitting closest to Holme either looked at him arrogantly or ignored him. Who ever heard of a thrall sitting at the king's table? But they were used to the king's sometimes doing what struck his fancy, in direct opposition to ancient custom and practice. In the next moment he might forget all this or turn the thrall over to the town authorities.

The king, however, was thinking constantly about what he would do when the meal was over and the thralls began running back and forth, taking away the wooden pails and tankards and cleaning up after the men. And without looking at anyone or asking anyone's advice, he took Holme with him to the silent, empty smithy and suggested he take charge of all the work that needed to be done at the farmstead. If Holme had any spare time he could make weapons he could use for bartering.

Holme had spent every moment at the table paying close attention to what was going on around him and trying to figure out what had happened. Had the king really been serious or did he invite the thrall to his table merely to amuse himself and his friends? Now he had no more doubts: the king wished to help him and Holme had done the right thing by seeking him out at the farmstead. He felt immense relief and happiness except for one thing – he still had to make arrangements for Ausi and Tora.

There were plenty of good tools lined up in rows in the king's smithy, and Holme examined them with interest. He greedily inhaled the smell of old soot, thinking how fortunate he would be to work here in peace and quiet, free from threats and persecution. Deep in his heart, something was still lodged like a thorn – he would not allow himself to forget freedom for others even if his own lot was good. A number of them had sacrificed their lives, and he owed it to them to keep working for the sake of those who still lived.

But he wasn't up to that battle just then; he longed for work and quiet. There still might be something he'd be able to do, though; the king was a good master and would understand. It was better to talk than to fight. No one had ever talked to him as the king had, a man who understood a great deal at a glance.

From the smithy, Holme could see across the cove to the forest on the other side, and the town was just barely visible in the distance. The king had told Holme about a house a little ways from the farmstead where he could live. And, to Holme's relief, the king had also asked if Holme had a wife and child and where they were. In response, Holme had pointed toward the mainland forest to the east.

It wasn't long before Holme was on his way home. The boat was there where he'd left it, and he didn't have to sneak up to it. Instead he walked boldly forward, dry branches breaking underfoot. He had no one to fear now. He rowed across the cove, watching the sun's dazzling rays on the water where the moon's red path had been many hours before. It was late autumn, but the day was like summer, and the surface of the water was as still as glass.

Two men and a woman stood by the jetty where he had borrowed the boat. While he was still a ways from the land, the men started threatening him for taking the boat. They yelled what would happen to him when he came ashore, and one of them picked up a heavy, dry club.

Holme rowed up, tied the boat to the jetty where he had found it, and stepped ashore. Although he had been awake all night and was tired, he stood silently before the irate men, and they stared just as silently back at him. The club sank down again, and the woman whispered his name in terror.

But nothing happened, and Holme moved on toward the edge of the forest. He didn't turn around to look back at the three people who were still standing by the jetty, staring after him, and no threats followed him. They were probably just happy to see him disappear. He didn't know them, but they had doubtlessly seen him in town and had heard the rumors about him when they were there to sell their fish.

He walked quickly through the forest, happy he hadn't been forced to strike the men down. He had fought many times, and he had killed a few men, but no one had ever won. The king, on the other hand, had come a long way with peaceful talk. Holme sensed a new way, a way where no one had to fight but where everyone could talk and come to terms. He could not see the way clearly, but the thought of it filled him with happiness. Perhaps one day the king would even understand the thoughts and feelings of thralls.

Pleasant thoughts filled Holme's head all the way back. He felt confident that nothing had happened to Ausi and Tora while he had been away. He had learned through the king that the warriors in town had refused to pursue him through the forest a second time, and that the will of the gods supported their decision. Maybe the charred god at the settlement had had a hand in this because Holme had put him back on the rock a few days ago. As he grew older, he no longer thought it completely impossible for the gods to get involved if they wanted to.

He clambered up the ridge in the dusk and walked by Stenulf's burial mound, made level by many years of pine needles settling between the stones. In a few more years the mound would be like a little hill. Stenulf had never shown himself after his death, regardless of how dark the night had been, and Holme had stopped looking toward his mound with fear. A powerful warrior like Stenulf had probably not stayed in the mound but rather had gone to the land of the dead.

No one came out of the cave when he approached it, but he saw that the branches covered the entrance as usual. That meant that Ausi and Tora had left of their own free will and would probably be back soon. Tonight they would all sleep in the cave, but early the next morning they would be off to the king's farmstead.

He took the branches away, crawled in, and started gathering his tools to take along. But then he remembered the good collection of tools in the king's smithy and considered the unpredictable future. He would leave his own tools hidden in the cave under branches and moss. They might be of use to him or someone else some day.

He sensed that someone was nearby and crawled out to look around. Everything was quiet, but behind a tree trunk something stuck out that didn't belong to the well-known landscape. Someone was there. He grabbed his ax and pretended to wander around haphazardly until he neared the tree. Then he pounced, his ax lifted in the air.

But it never fell. As he leaped, he heard a happy little shout and then someone came running. And there, under the ax, stood Ausi, her eyes opened wide. She and Tora had noticed that the branches were gone from the cave opening and hid to see who was there. They hadn't dared hope Holme would be back so soon.

They were overjoyed to see him in one piece and with a twinkle in his eye. They weren't used to seeing him so peaceful and happy. But they didn't ask what was going on; instead they just waited until he was ready to talk. Ausi went back to the slope for some fish they had caught and started to clean them. Holme made a fire, thinking how nice it was not to be afraid that the smoke would be seen and not to have to listen all the time for his pursuers. No riders came hunting him through the forest anymore and none would be coming. For the first time in many years he felt peaceful and at ease.

The three of them sat on the ground near the fire eating their grilled fish and bread. Holme told them everything. He saw his wife's face light up with joy, his daughter's with curiosity and excitement. And he momentarily let himself feel as they did. He didn't forget for a moment what he owed his fellow thralls, both the ones who had died in the fight for freedom and those who were still alive. But he could let it be for a while; he would see if, with the king's help, something could be done without violence and strife.

Tonight was their last night in the cave. It had protected and served them well more than once, but it looked as if they could manage without it from now on. But that was probably hoping for too much. The town, and even the king's farmstead, could be attacked and burned. Such things had happened often enough before.

After they lay down, he heard Ausi whispering in the darkness. He didn't pay much attention since he knew what she was doing. She was thanking Christ for the good fortune and asking Him for His protection in the future. It didn't do any harm anymore; she could just as well keep on praying. Many years ago she would talk out loud to Christ, but Holme had tired of listening there beside her and had asked her to be quiet. After that, she whispered or talked out loud only if she was alone. But she hadn't stopped.

A hint of moonbeam settled on the sticks and grass in the cave's entrance. The night promised to be like the one before so they'd have good weather for the journey. He just hoped the king would stand by his word. Now that Holme was in the cave and it was night, his good fortune that day seemed like a dream. Nothing like it had ever happened before.

He could hear that Ausi was still awake and he told her quietly that it might be a trap, that the king might summon his warriors to kill him when they arrived. It wouldn't matter so much if he were alone. But he kept imagining his wife and daughter as thralls, beaten and scorned because of him, and that caused him more anguish than anything ever had before.

Ausi calmed him down by pointing out that the king wouldn't be so deceitful. Besides, she reminded him, he had sat among the king's warriors that very same day. If the king had wanted to, he never would have let Holme out alive. And if things still turned out as Holme feared, then she and Tora would rather die with him than live in slavery. Christ would care for all three of them and they would enjoy peace with Him.

Holme listened to what she said with only half an ear. He had calmed down but decided to watch his step. If it was a trap, he'd make sure he wasn't the only one left lying on the battlefield. The muscles in his arms and legs tightened as he imagined the battle. He wasn't young any longer, but he could still hold his own in a fight or in work.

But the happy, tranquil thoughts returned. Before falling asleep, Holme saw the king's smithy among the birch trees on the slope, the lake glittering down below. He would show the friendly king what he could do once left in peace with his own work.

The women were still asleep when Holme crawled out of the cave into the dawn. The woods were totally quiet and a mist hung over the marshland below the ridge. It rolled halfway up the slope but the ridge's uppermost part was bathed in the early morning light. The sun would melt away the mist, and it was going to be a clear day.

He wanted to go to the settlement one last time. He didn't have anything more to do there; he just wanted to see it. It might be the last time. And it might be enjoyable to go there once without having to sneak around like a troll peering out from behind tree trunks. He looked hesitatingly at his ax but let it be. Instead he picked up a heavy stick with an iron point on it. It had been in the cave since the first summer he and Ausi had lived there and the point was red with rust. He could at least defend himself with that if a wolf or wild boar decided to attack. He hesitated a moment longer, then kneeled down for something a second time. It was a little grilled fish and a piece of bread. He looked almost ashamed as he hid them in his clothes.

It wasn't long before Holme was in the cold and raw mist. It got so thick at one point that he had to stop and feel his way forward. All he could see was an aspen branch sticking out of the mist, hung with a few yellow leaves dripping with moisture. But soon a light breeze came, revealing the treetops above him. Then the mist began glowing a yellowish-gold in the direction he was walking. The sun must be coming up.

Wet branches struck him everywhere, soon spotting his gray clothes with moisture. Beautiful, dew-laden spiderwebs spanned the path, and he crawled under or walked around them. A bird took off with a rush of wings, scaring a rabbit from its lair. Holme saw its bounding back legs for an instant, and then it was gone.

Nothing had changed at the settlement but he hadn't really expected it to. The fields would probably grow over again now, the buildings collapse, and that wasn't good. The ground was rich and many people could live there. But he couldn't do anything about it. The buildings would probably become a refuge for robbers and outlaws. That might be just as well, though. He knew outcasts better than others did and knew they often were people who didn't wish to do anyone any harm. They only had to defend themselves against injustice and mistreatment.

The charred wooden god was dimly visible through the sunlit mist, and Holme walked down to it. The god had been through quite a lot, but he was stubborn and strong. There he stood, years after the settlement had been burned and the owners were gone. Holme started growing fond of him; they were alike somehow. He took out the fish and bread to place on the stone, but they smelled good and he was hungry. The wooden god could share with him;

they could each have half. He divided the fish and the bread, laying half on the stone before him and eating the rest as he looked around. All was still. Only mild breezes came from the cove where seagulls laughed and screeched.

There wasn't anything worth taking from the settlement now. The ashes from the fire had long been overgrown with bushes and large plants, yellow and drooping now, stiff with cold, wet with dew. The mist still danced and played around the three burial mounds in the aspen grove, and Holme wondered if he would ever come back there.

He drank some water from the old spring before turning back. The spring was still gurgling, unconcerned about the settlement's desolation, and the stream from it swung left a short distance away. The hole where the water gathered was half-filled with mud.

The mist was gone; only a faint fog still hung above the surface of the water. Holme looked back from the edge of the forest with a strange feeling in his heart. The road beside him led to the farmstead where the young thrall and his woman had dared settle. He should let them know that they were in less danger than they were before, and so Holme decided to take that road when he and his family left later on that day. It would be good to see the man again who had stood by him through dangerous battles and whose craving for freedom was stronger than most others'. He and his woman had to know, too, that Holme wouldn't be in the cave anymore if they needed his help.

After one last look over the slope and lake, he returned to the cave where his wife and daughter joyfully awaited him.

From a distance they could hear the sound of ax blows from the farmstead, but they soon fell silent. Holme knew that the thrall had discovered them and hidden to see who was coming, friend or foe. He soon recognized them and rushed from his hiding place with childlike enthusiasm.

Everything had gone well the first few days and he proudly showed them what he had already accomplished. No enemies had shown up, and his face beamed when he heard that none would be coming from town either. He wasn't afraid of pirates and highwaymen; such men had always been around and you simply had to cope with that. And he was a freeman now. The old chieftain's relatives were bound not to return, and besides, all that were left were Svein, the stiff-necked boy, and his horrible witch of a mother. They would surely stay in town forever.

Holme felt deeply satisfied seeing a thrall free and happy. He had done more work than he would ever have done as a slave. This showed again that freedom was a boon that everyone should have. More work would be done and done happily, as it had been here, instead of with grumbling and a desire to cleave the master's skull with an ax.

But many thralls had lost their lives so this one could be free. They had been slaughtered like dogs. Freedom could not walk that road; there had to be another one.

Then Holme thought about the king again. Maybe he would understand all thralls as he had understood Holme and would see that they would work and fight better if they were free.

The thrall's wife hurried to get food ready, and soon everyone was sitting around the split-log table. The thrall couple showed them the grain they had stored up and the field they had already sown. They planned to trap animals for the winter and barter for goods with their furs as people had always done. And they'd brew their own beer. If he let his beard grow, no one in the town would recognize him, and in a few winters he would get some help for the work and the hunting. The thrall laughed, clapping his wife's swelling stomach with his big hand.

Their joy refreshed Holme, and he no longer felt such deep sorrow for those who had given up their lives. Had the dead held out and stayed away from town, they too could have known freedom and happiness. But when they had no one to lead them, they soon lost their courage. A man must be able to live alone, without a leader.

Holme would much rather have stayed in the forest a freeman than go to the king's farmstead as a smith. He knew that now. But he couldn't do it. If he didn't do what the king wanted, the hunt would start all over again, and then the young thrall and his family would be killed or driven away. Too many people knew that he had stood by Holme and had killed a number of freemen. He had to be saved; he was the first thrall to be free and happy.

Holme soon moved on with his wife and daughter. He wanted to reach the king's farmstead while it was still daylight. The former thralls followed them on the road and both families promised to visit each other. And if either was in some kind of trouble, they would come to the other for help. Holme immediately started thinking about how he might help them out of various scrapes, since it didn't occur to him that he might ever need to call on them. He had never asked anyone to help him. Thralls couldn't and, until now, no one with power except the king had befriended him.

The families parted in the forest where sun and shadow, warmth and coolness, clashed on that clear autumn day. But Holme walked on with a lighter heart. He had seen one small consequence of his long, bitter fight. It wasn't much, but those two free, happy human beings showed how things could be. There was no limit to the land to cultivate; the woods were full of animals, and the lakes full of fish. Slavery just didn't seem necessary, even though every freeman said it was. He would tell the king all this when the time came.

The thrall couple's parting call rang through the forest, then died away in the direction of their farmstead. Ausi and Tora talked cheerfully, wondering what it would be like at the king's farmstead. They could see that Holme was deep in thought, so they didn't disturb him. They never took that gentle expression on his dark face for granted and were always glad to see it.

As they approached the fishing village opposite the king's farmstead, Holme remembered that they had to borrow a boat. That might present a problem. He had no desire for a confrontation; he felt calm and happy after the visit with his friends.

But he didn't have to worry. From a distance they saw people gathering by one of the jetties and someone waving to them from a boat. Holme walked closer and quickly saw his hunch was right. The king had sent a boat for them with a thrall to row it. He had been waiting there half the day.

The people in the fishing village stared at Holme and his family with excitement. They had heard so much about them, and now there they stood. It was hard for the men to believe that the powerfully built man with the calm eyes could be the dangerous, violent man whom they had heard tales about, but who was now under the king's protection. They looked too at his beautiful wife and black-eyed daughter. A few people remembered them from when they had lived in town and Holme had led the uprising against the Christians.

As they watched the boat set out with the smith family, they began chattering eagerly among themselves. Nothing like this had ever happened before: the king had taken an outlaw into his service. They'd have to wait and see what would happen now, but this probably meant that the days of peace were at an end.

The king's thrall rowed with mighty strokes to impress them, and he glowed when Holme said a few appreciative words. It was the first time the smith had been rowed in a boat like a chieftain, and he wasn't really happy about it. But Ausi was and already felt that she almost belonged to the king's court. Tora looked with simultaneous curiosity and mistrust toward the king's farmstead, reminding Ausi once again that her resemblance to her father wasn't just physical. He too directed his face toward the farmstead, a threatening wrinkle lodged between his eyebrows. If this was a trick, he was ready. It would be a tough fight, but Ausi and Tora would die with Holme. That didn't frighten Ausi. Christ would meet them and understand everything. He had to know that Holme had never chosen to do any harm, that he befriended the weak just like Christ Himself did.

She stretched out her hand and caressed Holme's cheek. He looked at her and understood. Yes, if it came to a fight, it was best to do what she wanted: kill them both. If he couldn't do it, Ausi would. She and their daughter had tasted freedom; it had taken root in them and they would never again be thralls.

For the first time in his life, he reached out and returned his wife's caress. He saw her eyes gleam as never before while Tora looked wonderingly at both of them.

All three were completely calm when they stepped ashore at the king's jetty.

Svein's mother was seething with rage and despair as she walked toward her hut after the warriors had refused to go to the mainland and kill Holme. She didn't dare now go back to rebuild the settlement for her son. If Holme was on the loose in the forest, they wouldn't have a safe moment.

She still had some silver left that she had hidden for the rebuilding. The Christians wouldn't wheedle any more out of her. They said that Christ would help her for nothing, but they still came begging for His church. The priests probably kept whatever they collected, and new ones would be coming in the spring. These last monks couldn't take living among the heathens either and had gained permission to return home.

Beside her stood a large, beautiful house that she looked at enviously every time she walked outside. It belonged to a woman and her daughter, the town's richest inhabitants. While the woman's husband was alive, he had overtaken many vessels on the sea, killed their crews, and plundered them. Consequently, he was much esteemed, and people still greeted his wife and daughter with respect.

The rich woman and her daughter were Christians, and they had given a great deal to the Christian priests. The chieftain visited them often, and when the priests left, they held services there with singing and talks about Christ. Svein's mother sometimes thought about joining them, but she still resented the chieftain too much for letting Holme live. She was surprised to see Svein listening to the songs without a scoff or a frown. He had gotten more even-tempered recently and seemed to have something on his mind. He went off with the warriors at the fortress every day to learn how to use weapons.

One morning Svein's mother walked down to the harbor to buy some fish. The fishermen came in early with their night catches, and many kinds of fish were flopping and splashing in the boats' bilge water. As she sorted through the catch, she heard Holme's name and her ears perked up.

Someone said that Holme had become the king's smith and lived there with his family. When she grasped what she had heard, she shrieked with rage, dropped the fish, and clutching up her

47

skirt sped off toward town. The startled people in the harbor watched her go and isolated laughter broke out. The news spread quickly and soon people in town were talking about it everywhere.

Svein's mother ran straight to the chieftain's house, which lay close to the Christian quarters. She heard singing from the church and looked in. A handful of people were in the pews closest to the front singing a morning hymn to Christ. She was going to rush up to the chieftain, who was leading the hymn, anyway, but a guard stopped her and shoved her out the door. She stood outside still sobbing with rage.

After a while the few churchgoers left and went to their work. The chieftain came out last, and the woman immediately began railing loudly about what she had just heard. The chieftain listened in surprise but didn't believe her. Some other people from the harbor, however, soon corroborated what she had said. The chieftain listened to them in silence, wondering once more how long that thrall would be allowed to live and bring unrest to the people in town. The king had to release him and he would be put on trial at the assembly.

The chieftain calmed the woman down by saying that the king could not oppose the people's will. Besides, the whole thing might be one of the king's ploys for capturing this dangerous man. In either case, she should calm down. Holme would never again return to the mainland forest and no one there would have to live in fear of him any longer. Finally he promised to visit the king that day and find out what was going on.

When Svein heard the news he snapped out of the lethargy that had engulfed him. For quite some time he had remained silent when his mother came complaining angrily and viciously about Holme and his family. But he often thought about them. He was still afraid of Holme, but he let his thoughts circumvent him and settle on Tora. He still felt he had a claim on her. He was almost a full-grown man now, and he needed a young woman thrall before he could get the settlement in order and find a wife.

These thoughts intensified once he heard his mother's story, and he walked up a hill to look toward the king's farmstead. So, there she was now, the slender, bad-tempered girl. If she came to town without her father, he would have her, rape her. He could lure her into the house or into the woods outside town. He had seen a great deal that time he had wandered around out there. Alien sailors, showing no respect for the family burial mounds, lay out there with women after eating and getting drunk on beer or mead. He watched it all with aching desire, but one day it would be his turn.

But winter was coming and nothing would happen. There were long days ahead in the house's darkness broken only by the fire-light flickering from the hearth. The snow would be deep and the ice would roar round about the island. The midwinter sacrifice was the only thing to look forward to. Then maybe Holme would come to town with his daughter – if he was lucky enough not to be sentenced to death at the assembly, that is.

While Svein stood looking toward the distant, royal farmstead, the view gradually faded and tiny snowflakes started dancing around him. This was the first snow of the autumn, and it seemed to come in response to his morose thoughts about winter. The squall rolled over the island, soon making the north sides of the burial mounds in the ancestral meadow glisten. A woman from town came walking that way. He recognized her. The whole town knew that she carried food to her husband's mound every day. She had placed a bowl in a hollow she had dug in the mound. Every day it was toppled over and empty, which made her believe that her husband had eaten the food. The Christian priests had told her that animals had, but she scoffed at them and kept up her practice.[4]

Svein watched her walk by. She was still young and looked happy. The bowl was steaming and she walked quickly, kicking up her skirt. She probably wanted to get to the mound before the soup got cold.

Driven by curiosity and some less definite feeling, Svein followed her. She didn't turn around, so from behind the closest mound, he could see her put the bowl in place as she talked in a soft, encouraging voice. When she bent forward he stared hungrily at her legs, exposed partway up the calves.

The snow-squall had passed and the sun poked through the clouds. The bare limbs of the birch trees started dripping; the snowflakes were melting and the land of burial mounds glowed an autumn yellow. The woman walked home without having noticed the stiff-necked youth behind the mound. She'd come back again the next day around the same time.

Svein stood there, not knowing what to do. The idea of going home to his mother, who was always angry and railing about something or someone, wasn't very appealing. He looked around, suddenly noticing movement in some small bushes nearby. He soon saw a pair of cold eyes observing him.

He walked slowly away so that the animal would venture out. The eyes followed him as long as they could, then wandered anxiously about for a moment. With back lowered, the wild cat sneaked toward the grave and the bowl of food. Svein realized that this wasn't the first time it had dined on the dead man's food.

But it was still too hot today. The cat snarled, pawed at the bowl gently, and sat down to wait. It turned and stared mistrustfully at

4. Schön (*Fridegård och forntiden*, pp. 148–49) reports that bowls of the type the woman uses have been found in the burial mounds at Birka.

Svein's motionless head behind the mound. But after a while it re-laxed and tested the bowl again with its paw.

Svein was as curious as a little boy and realized that the Christian priest was right: animals had eaten the man's food. This cat was well-fed and probably came around every day.

Some magpies smelled the food too and were chattering anxiously in the nearby trees; the cat shot an occasional cold, malevolent glance at them. Finally it got up and stuck its nose into the bowl. By its movements, it seemed to be lapping up some of the broth. After a while it extracted a piece of meat, sat down, and started chewing, its head turning from side to side.

Svein hoped the dead man would reach out and kill the cat, strangle it or something, but nothing happened. So he got bored and shouted. The cat dashed a couple of steps away but turned and retrieved the meat when it saw it was only a human being making the noise. Then it slid off between a couple of burial mounds, and the magpies moved in. When Svein looked around, there was a commotion of wings and flapping tails surrounding the bowl. It would surely be tipped over and empty for the woman the next day. He decided to hide again to watch her. Maybe her skirt would slide higher so he could see more leg.

A new snow-squall came from the lake, obscuring his vision, and he began walking faster. The fortress disappeared, first behind the whirling flakes and then behind the buildings in town. Winter had arrived – long, dark winter.

After promising Svein's mother to visit the king and bring Holme to trial, the chieftain began to have doubts. He wasn't sure the people were behind him in this matter, and without their support he could never win.

He walked to the fortress to talk with the warriors gathered there. They showed absolutely no interest. If the king had taken the skilled smith into his service, it was nobody's business. Everyone knew that Holme was the best smith in town, perhaps even in the whole kingdom. The king obviously knew what he was doing.

The warriors yawned through their beards and talked among themselves about other things, paying no more attention to the chieftain. This was all very odd. They hadn't been able to capture the smith – just one man – and so they gave up. It must be because he was a thrall. They surely couldn't be afraid of him.

The chieftain went back to town and talked with some of the most prominent merchants. They were indifferent, too. They talked about the days when they could get proper smithwork done at a reasonable cost. If the king had taken the smith into his service, that didn't concern them. Holme had done them no harm and they didn't want to see him dead. They would not ask that he be sentenced since they didn't even know that he was guilty of everything people said about him.

It was only the Christians who backed the chieftain. They thought that such a terrible criminal, and a heathen besides, had to die and be lost for eternity. Hadn't he once desecrated their holy church and divided their grain among the starving heathens? Wasn't he Christ's greatest enemy in town and the surrounding district?

But there were too few Christians; they couldn't force the issue, so the chieftain postponed his trip to the king. It was autumn now and everyone was growing listless and sullen because of the approaching winter. Once winter had arrived, the atmosphere would be different.

When the angry woman came to complain, that's what he told her: she would have her justice in the spring and would be able to rebuild the settlement. During the winter, she should gather thralls to cut lumber and carry it out on crude sleds. The chieftain had seen the settlement when he had hunted Holme and knew it was in a good location and had rich fields. It was worth rebuilding. Christ would protect it from attacks and plundering if the woman would let herself and her son be baptized.

The woman promised to renounce the gods of her fathers if Christ would help her. But in her heart, she knew she would keep sacrificing to the wooden gods. No one had to know. After all, they had helped her father, her husband, and her many times before. She didn't dare turn her back on them.

The chieftain was pleased to see the woman calm down and go home. She had the law on her side and could demand her rights at the assembly. It would be a peaceful winter in the meantime, and there would be some way out come spring. New priests would arrive, and the Christian work would go forward with renewed vigor. That was the message he had recently received from the Christian bishop, together with the admonition to hold out.

The king could have his smith for the winter, but the people would decide his fate in the spring. Such had always been the law of the land. The king couldn't act arbitrarily in matters affecting everybody.

Everything was ready for the winter now. Everyone had gathered stores of food, and everywhere you could hear the pigs grunting in their stalls. They would be fattened for the winter sacrifice. The chieftain had been around those winters when the food had run out, and he and his men had had to cross the snow-covered expanses of ice to find meat on the mainland. Like black dots, shivering men could be seen fishing through holes everywhere on the vast, snow-covered ice field.

At the mainland farmsteads, the chieftain bought live animals with the merchants' money – cows, sheep, goats. The next day, their new owner crossed the ice, leading the reluctant animals with him. Farmers with grain and other goods to sell followed along on their sleds, set up a market on the ice, and demanded a high price. As long as the ice was there, no merchants from foreign lands appeared.

The harvest had been bad that year because of the blight the wooden gods had visited on the grain. The heathens blamed Christ, and the priest had fled for his life. If he had stayed the winter, and the heathens had begun to starve, no one could have saved him from being sacrificed to the wooden gods, not even Christ Himself. This priest was not one to crave martyrdom. The first one had been, the one who had been slaughtered at the great spring sacrifice many years before.

The march sun beat down on the king's fields, which were almost powder dry. The only place the ground was still dark with moisture was in the indentations, and there was still a little snow water trickling in the furrows. Out in the forest, the north sides of the trees still had flecks of grainy snow on them, peppered with pine needles and dry blades of grass.

In a couple of days the spring plowing could begin, and preparations were already underway. The queen had saved a large, dry roll that had been baked for the winter sacrifice, and one of the barrels still had some beer in it. During the spring plowing, both man and beast would partake of that luck-bringing food.

The field below the birch grove where Holme lived was directly in the sun and so already dry. The ditch banks glowed with yellow flowers that would close up and disappear when the sun went down.

The smith's family had passed their calmest winter – no one chasing them, no hunger, no cold. Sometimes a rumor rippled through the farmstead about Holme's having to appear before the spring assembly, but no one mentioned it to him. The king visited the smithy almost daily, pleased about all the weapons and other goods for barter that Holme forged on the anvil. He talked with the smith frequently and became more and more convinced that he was a decent human being who didn't want to hurt anyone, who wouldn't attack unless he was forced to.

There had been some disturbances in town a couple of times during the late winter. The heathens accused the chieftain of disrespecting people's rights to the store of food. The Christians weren't suffering, and someone had seen them carrying burdens from the storehouse at night. But when the heathens confronted them about this, they answered that Christ had given them food. If you believed in Him and accepted baptism, He would supply your needs.

But the heathens would not be fooled. They kept watch and saw the chieftain dispensing grain and meat to his people, and they became enraged. Some messengers were sent across the ice to the king, saying that if justice wasn't done soon, the people would be driven into a murderous frenzy against all the Christians.

The king returned to town with the messengers and managed to restore peace. He gave whatever food he could spare from his own stores and reminded the people that as soon as the water opened, merchant ships would arrive with all kinds of goods and exchange them for the Norsemen's skins and metalwork. The king wasn't very happy about the thought that new priests would be coming then too. The heathens' bitterness against them was greater than before, and it could cost the priests their lives at any time. The ruler in the southern lands was powerful; he could forbid his people to come to Scandinavia with their goods if his missionaries got killed.

The king thought about these matters as he strolled through his fields. He was a peaceful man and would prefer seeing the Christians left in peace as long as they did the same to the wooden gods. He couldn't see much difference between them and Christ. Christ was made of wood, too, and hung above the altar in the church. There was talk in town of miracles he had done, like healing the sick, but the king hadn't seen it with his own eyes. Besides, one god had been in this land longer than human memory – a god who had healed their forefathers – and he could be just as good as Christ.[5]

Thralls were working in the field outside Holme's house now, preparing it for sowing. They had their hoods off in the sunshine and shouted lightheartedly at the work animals. The foreman stood on a ditch bank supervising, and the hammer rang in the smithy.

Everything was coming to life. The spring ice was still there, white and porous, but it had broken loose from the land, making room for the pikes to surface in the grass by the shore. In the distance, you could see a surging band of blue water. Carpenters were busy with the ships, sending the sound of frequent hammer blows from the harbor. One of them would stop for a minute now and then to fetch nails or fittings from the smithy.

The men longed for the sea when the spring winds started ruffling their hair and beards. They kept examining their weapons and visiting Holme in the smithy. And the thought the king had had the past autumn about conducting a raid across the ocean returned and grew stronger. His kingdom was poorer now than ever before and so was he. Once the sowing and the other spring work was done, they would have to set sail.

A few days later, the ground was ready for sowing. The foreman was up early, drenching the work animals' fodder with beer before they were brought from their stalls. That would insure them

5. I.e., the Norse god, Thor.

health and strength for the coming year, and they would have plentiful offspring.

Meanwhile, the thralls carried a vat of beer into the field and placed it next to the seed grain. They looked expectantly toward the farmstead now and then, which was just coming to life. Some of the king's men went into his court and came out carrying a large wooden god on a pole. They took him into the field and put him down near the vat of beer. There he stood, grinning a crooked smile, his long, rough-hewn organ jutting diagonally up into the air.

More and more men and women left the farmstead to gather in the field. The thralls stood off by themselves, and Holme brought Tora and Ausi from the smithy. Ausi, wanting to distance herself from the thralls, edged closer to the freemen, but Holme yanked her back. She smiled a little shamefacedly while Holme thought that she always wanted to make herself out to be better than she was. She was a thrall, and she should stand with the others until all of them were free. Some curious children had gathered in a group, but when the foreman came, he shouted at them to go away. They reluctantly walked off just over the top of a hill. They could see everything from there.

Only the king and queen were missing. The men working on the ships stopped to watch what was happening on the field, and all grew quiet. Only the song of the lark filled the air.

Everyone watched as the king and queen approached from the farmstead. The king held a branch covered with small, fresh leaves. It had been kept in some water inside the building so it would be ready for the sowing. The king looked around and nodded in approval. Everything was right. The gods had provided good weather, so they had to be pleased with the sacrifices he had offered in the spring.

The foreman, who would sow the grain himself, walked up to

the king. There were several beer tankards beside the vat, and a couple of women thralls were busy filling them. A horn belonging to the king stood there, too, but this the queen filled herself and handed to him with a smile. The foreman and highest-ranking warriors likewise had horns, which the queen or their own women filled and handed to them.

When everyone was quiet, the king dipped the branch in the beer and let it rain over the grinning wooden god, soaking it completely. The beer trickled down and was swallowed immediately by the earth, which had opened its womb to receive the offering – a good omen.

Then tankards were passed out among the hall servants and highest-ranking thralls. The rest – the big crowd of thrall laborers – rushed to the vat at a signal from the queen. They filled their wooden ladles and gulped wildly, both men and women. The children on the hill had moved closer. They didn't care anymore that they could be seen. They just stared in amazement and excitement at what was going on.

After drinking from his horn, the king dipped the green birch branch in the beer again and sprinkled his smiling queen. Then it was her turn, and she sprinkled the brown liquid all over the king. The foreman was next and then each of the high-ranking warriors. The thralls were standing off by themselves in a group, but a sparkle had come into their eyes because of the beer. The king walked around, smiling a friendly smile through his beard, pouring beer on all of them.

When the preliminaries were over, the king motioned for the sowing bushel to be hung around the foreman's neck. He had emptied his large horn and wasn't too steady on his feet, a fact that made everybody laugh. He soon regained his balance, though, and walked along, tossing the golden grain from side to side onto the ground. Several thralls followed him and covered the seed with rakes. As they did so, they yelled and screamed at the birds that were trying to feed on the grain as it fell.

Holme was glad to see that the king did not differentiate much between freemen and thralls. They all got beer; it was only the container – horn or tankard – that varied. And they all got sprinkled. If everyone treated their thralls like the king did, freedom might develop on its own without violence and conflict. These thralls were happy and well-fed, but the ones at other farmsteads weren't so lucky.

The foreman kept sowing but would stop occasionally for a slug of beer while the thralls refilled the basket. A butterfly, awakened too early, flew erratically along the furrow, fluttered to the vat, and landed in the sun on the sweet, moist wood.

A boat had docked at the jetty, and some men were walking toward the farmstead. The laborers looked, wondering if they could be the new Christian priests, and the king walked back toward the farmstead after leaving orders for another vat of beer for the workers. He would be back soon. When he was out of sight, some of the thralls sat down on a pile of rocks with their tankards. The rocks had been there long before they had, and the lowest layer had sunk halfway into the earth. Their fathers had probably unearthed the rocks and piled them there. When the foreman approached the pile on his next round, some of the thralls hesitantly stood up, but the more tipsy ones sat still. The foreman looked at them, but the beer had put him in a good mood so he left them alone. He knew that by dusk no one would either hear or care about anything he said. This was a day of celebration and belonged to the fertility god. That night, after the fields had been sown, it would be the women's turn. They knew it; their eyes sparkled and they blushed when they looked at the men.

After the first field was sown, the one by the smithy, Holme tired of being out in the sun and went back inside. No one tried to stop him; they were used to his doing whatever he wanted and obeying only the king. Ausi and Tora returned to the house in the birch grove, but didn't feel like working. There was something in the air, so they soon went outside again and sat on a rock where they could watch the people in the fields. They saw the thralls dipping their ladles into the beer whenever the foreman's back was turned.

One thrall emerged from the forest driving a wagon with crude wheels and loaded with wood and dry twigs. He unloaded the wagon on a grassy area near the farmstead where a bonfire would burn that night. As he worked, a woman thrall appeared carrying a tankard that she handed to him. He drank and then grabbed hold of her, making her laugh and wriggle in his arms. Ausi knew they'd be together later that night.

In the afternoon, the work was finished. The wooden god was carried through the newly planted fields, and everyone followed in the procession. They were all tired but soon would rest. On the way back, a couple of thralls picked up the empty beer vat and both god and vat were placed near the woodpile.

Holme started home from the smithy. All day long he had been thinking about the boat that had appeared earlier. He had been free and clear of the Christians for a while but wondered if it would start all over again. Bad things always happened when they were around, no matter what they said about peace. They divided friend from friend, wife from husband, and blood was always running wherever they went, despite their saying that they didn't offer human sacrifices.

Their boat was still there, but they would probably go back the same day. If he had figured them right, they wouldn't dare stay on a night like this. The king wouldn't want them here either. The celebration concerned only the people at the farmstead and whoever else the king invited.

It was rumored from town that many Christians had turned away from their faith during the winter. That was good, but these new monks would start gathering followers again, and the king would surely permit them to preach freely.[6] When they had come to the king's farmstead, they had thralls behind them carrying various objects. They must be gifts to this king from the king who ruled the monk's homeland.

Holme had stopped in the birch grove while he thought about all this. The scent of spring was in the air, and some downy-gray flower buds were pushing their way up near his feet. He recognized what they were and knew they would eventually open into deep blue cups with yellow specks at the bottom. When the petals were gone, they would be left standing like glittering gray spiders in the wind.

Like most people, he longed to leave there even though he had everything he could want. Something was beckoning him – the forest, his old thrall friends, the cave, the settlement. Someday he

6. It is not clear which – if any – of the monks described in *Vita Anskarii* Frideård intends these two to be, since he has not been following Rimbert closely. In 844, Gautbert, the nephew Ansgar had consecrated bishop, was driven from Sweden. Seven years later, Ansgar, then the archbishop of Hamburg with all of Scandinavia under his jurisdiction, sent a hermit named Ardgar to Birka (*Anskar,* chapter 19, p. 62). In that same year the chieftain Herigar died (chapter 19, p. 69) and, shortly thereafter, Ardgar left Sweden (chapter 20, p. 73). In 853 Ansgar returned for his second mission to Sweden, which then had a new king, Olaf (chapter 26, p. 89). He left a nephew of Gautbert's, Erimbert, in charge of the mission when he returned to Hamburg in 854 (chapter 28, p. 95). In 854 or 855, Gautbert sent a priest named Ansfrid to join Erimbert; they stayed for three to four years and were followed by Rimbert (chapter 33, pp. 103–4). The mission remained dormant after Ansgar's death in 865.

would ask the king if he could leave for a few days, and he would visit the young thrall and his woman at the relatives' farmstead. That would make it easier to stay on the island during the summer.

The large gate at the king's farmstead suddenly opened, and a number of figures came walking out. Holme recognized the long gowns on two of them. It had been a long time since he had first seen such garments, and many priests had been killed or driven off. But they never gave up. The best thing now for everyone would be for those two to be chased off immediately.

Holme also recognized the town's most powerful man, the gray-bearded, Christian chieftain who, with his men, had hunted Holme through the forests. There Holme had an enemy; he could feel it in the air. In that instant of recognition, the chieftain turned toward Holme, possibly even seeing the dark figure among the white tree trunks.

Something told Holme that the battle wasn't over yet, and he was somehow glad. He had longed for peace and work during the autumn and winter, and he had gotten what he wanted. But he was getting restless. Just like a woman, he thought, shaking his head.

Once he had tried to talk with the king about freedom for thralls, but he couldn't find the right words. Besides, the king's thralls were almost free anyway, so the king couldn't or wouldn't understand what Holme was getting at. He had looked at him strangely, then changed the subject to the smithy.

It was really for the best, then, if something new happened. He couldn't walk around here his whole life while countless thralls were tormented and some even killed by their masters. It was possible that a good many of them had heard about Holme and were expecting his help. And so he felt more sharply than ever before what he had to do: help. Everything was calm and peaceful here, and that's why he had become restless. He would wait until the right time, though. Christian priests had returned and they would doubtlessly put an end to the tranquillity that had lasted through the winter.

The boat set out, several pairs of oars flashing rhythmically in and out of the water. Those sending it off walked back to the farmstead; Holme walked toward his house. His wife and daughter were on a rock outside, and they looked at him with a mixture of hope and anxiety – would they get to join the festivities in the king's courtyard?

Toward evening, the whole farmstead came alive. The king and all his retinue dressed in colorful, gold-embroidered garments, the thralls who owned decent clothes put them on, and the queen and her companions made up their eyes with something from the king's physician that made their eyes look large and lustrous.

Men and women thralls were scampering everywhere, arranging for food and drink for the feast. Squealing and grunting could be heard from the pigsty where two thralls were holding onto a medium-sized pig as they carefully scrubbed it. They talked about the upcoming feast and would slap the pig on the snout whenever it squealed too loudly. The young women kept smiling at each other as they did their chores. They had waited all winter for this night.

At dusk, a big ship sailed into the harbor, bringing friends and relatives of the royal couple. The men had donned glistening armor, and the women, richly adorned clothes. Their thralls carried the stores ashore, and the setting sun cast its last gleaming rays on the illustrious train as it moved up toward the farmstead. The thralls ogled the noble women, thinking about the lascivious chaos of the approaching night. There had been a time or two when a thrall had sneaked up to them, and they couldn't see or didn't care who was loosening their clasps because of the beer and darkness. And a powerful warrior would often secretly find a woman thrall whose young body or beautiful face enticed him. Later, no one would see whether he had her with or without her consent. The thrall women knew all this and they glanced furtively at the warriors.

When the bonfire was lit, Holme walked out of his house with his wife and daughter. They had bathed and changed clothes. He hadn't planned on going to the feast, but he finally had to give in to the looks of two pairs of plaintive eyes. Ausi hadn't said anything. She was thinking about the sacrificial feast many years before when the frenzy had made her follow another man into a clump of pine trees. This time they would only stand to one side to watch, and she wouldn't drink anything that would make her head feel strange and cause her body to want a man who didn't belong to her.

Before they had walked to the end of the short path, the fire was already blazing high, crackling through the branches and wood. It lit up the tables and benches, and happy faces emerged from all directions out of the darkness into the firelight. The door of the king's farmstead was standing open, revealing a big fire in the hearth in the middle of the hall, with a gigantic cauldron hanging over it. A sturdy pole had been driven into the ground just outside the door, and a steady stream of thralls carried food and drink from the building to the festival area.

The king's thralls didn't have to wait that night until their masters had finished feasting and then devour the leftovers. The king had decreed that they should have their own table. Holme thought once more that if everyone treated his thralls as the king did, it would be easy to solve a pressing problem. But no one was like him, neither heathen nor Christian.

The sight of the fire, the tables, and the happy faces brought to mind the great sacrificial feast of long ago at the heathen temple.

He looked mistrustfully at Ausi's face. As then, her eyes were glowing with expectation, and in the firelight she looked like a young girl. But she was smarter now and wouldn't run off with someone else. Besides, he wouldn't let her or Tora out of his sight. When the men got drunk, they'd grab the first woman who came along and be pleased and excited by the struggling and screaming.

The king came out and surveyed the yard. His clothes were embroidered in gold, and a short, pearl-inlaid sword hung at his belt. He walked around the courtyard to inspect the preparations, even visiting the thralls' table. Holme stood in the background, and the king approached him. He asked Holme in a friendly voice to see that the thralls were treated well and justly. All the food and drink they needed would be sent to their table. When the king saw that everything was ready, he went back into his house.

The fire blazed higher, sending a flickering light onto the wooden god standing beside the sacrificial pole. More and more people milled around waiting for the celebration to begin, while the two thralls at the pigsty kept an eye on the freshly washed pig so it wouldn't get muddy again. It had finally calmed down and was now standing there blinking patiently at the fire in the yard. People teemed and swarmed in the firelight.

The king emerged again, followed by his closest advisors. The noise died down, and everyone gathered around the pole. There were a number of bronze and iron objects lying on a bench.

The king looked toward the sty, and the thralls responded to the signal. The pig squealed protractedly as it was carried, more than led, down the slope to the place of slaughter. The thralls then lifted it up, rolled it over onto its back, and grabbed hold of its frantically kicking legs.

The king signaled the foreman, who was still dressed in his work clothes. He took one of the knives, made a calculation, then cut the pig's throat. His wife held a bronze ladle under the wound, then emptied it into a bucket while the thralls repositioned the animal so blood wouldn't spill on the ground. The pig wheezed, its kicking weakened, and its bristly white eyes gradually closed in death.

The king took the branch he had used in the morning's ceremony, dipped it in the blood, and splashed blood all over the wooden god. As he did so, the foreman, with the thralls' help, hung the carcass on the sacrificial pole. The blood looked black in the flickering firelight, and the dogs prowled around greedily, sometimes dashing off and barking furiously at the green eyes that flashed and disappeared in the thickets. The stray cats had been enticed by the smell of blood, too.

The god had had his desires satisfied, so everyone could breathe a little easier. Now it was their turn. The king washed his hands in water a woman thrall poured over them and dried them on the towel another thrall had ready. Then in a loud voice he invited people to the table, and all kinds of figures came from various directions into the firelight. A thrall stood guard at the sacrificial pole with a big stick to keep the dogs away from the sacrifice. He looked jealously toward the thralls' table, clenching his teeth, and a younger woman thrall looked back. She would doubtlessly make sure he didn't lack anything during his watch.

Everyone sat down and picked up their horns or tankards at a signal from the king. Before lifting his horn to his lips, the king loudly promised rich offerings for the gods if they would stand by him. He named both of them, the one in the firelight beside them and the one in the darkness of the temple who gave good fortune in battle.[7] The king mentioned his plans for a raid that spring, and

7. I.e., the Norse gods, Freyr and Thor.

the rows of warriors murmured approvingly. After a quiet winter, they longed for the sea and adventure. Finally, the king named a few minor deities who watched over the harvest, the animals, house and home.[8]

Simultaneous preparations for the spring feast were going on in town as well. Svein wandered around watching but had no desire to take part. He had grown during the winter and was now half a head taller than his mother, who was a tall woman.

Svein was glad it was spring and had already decided to ask the king if he could go along on the raid he had heard rumors about in town. There'd still be plenty of time for rebuilding the old settlement, something his mother talked about daily. Or she could do it without him, for that matter.

From old habit, he walked up that spring day to the burial mounds to look toward the king's farmstead. He hadn't seen any member of Holme's family during the winter, neither at the feast nor at the big market on the ice. They probably still didn't dare show themselves in town. The spring assembly would meet soon, and his mother had already reminded the chieftain about her right to the smith's wife and daughter.

The year-old grass on the burial mounds had dried up, but new green shoots were sprouting on the south sides. There were yellow flowers glistening here and there, and he recognized them from previous springs at the settlement. The wind from the lake felt cooler here than it did in town.

He remembered the woman who carried food to her dead husband and walked toward the mound. There was the hollow and

8. These gods are difficult to identify but are probably associated with Freyr. See H. R. Ellis Davidson, *Gods and Myths of Northern Europe* (Harmondsworth: Penguin Books, 1964), pp. 103 ff.

the overturned bowl. A few small bones looked fresh so the woman probably still came there every day. He waited a while. It was the same time of day that he had seen her the previous autumn. Some magpies were sitting in the birch trees seeming to wait, and the cat with its cold eyes might be lurking nearby, too.

Happy voices and shouts were carried on the wind from the harbor. He had heard that many of the town's most important people would go to the king's feast. He knew what went on during such occasions, and a thought came like a flash, making his face blanch, then flush. The smith's daughter, Tora, was at the king's farmstead, and she was as good as grown. Someone would surely take her that night. Even her father couldn't save her if one of the king's nobles wanted her, and she might even want to be part of it all.

His blood started boiling with simultaneous rage and arousal. His clothes got tight, so he had to keep changing positions. That girl was his, and no one had a right to touch her. He imagined her struggling with another man, only finally to succumb, and he didn't know what to do. Should he ask those getting ready to go to the king's farmstead if he could go along? No, they wouldn't pay any attention to him, just drive him ignominiously away.

The cool wind passed over the mounds and rustled among the darkening flower stalks from the previous summer. A mighty stone, raised by his forefathers who had lived on the island before the town had even existed, stood atop one of the smaller mounds. It must be a powerful warrior who was buried there.

Svein calmed down but couldn't stop thinking about Tora and the sacrificial feast. He wanted to be there to see what happened. He could think about Holme now without the shudder he had once felt since he had been told many times that Holme wouldn't bother anyone unless he was attacked or provoked. Svein would have a stiff neck as long as he lived, but he didn't think about that. He only wanted revenge for it when his mother poured out her bitter hatred for the thrall's family.

Many people were walking among the burial mounds today. There were sacrificial stones in several places, and their hollows would be filled before evening. The cats, dogs, and birds would have a good day.

A woman passed through the gate, and he watched her in anticipation. It was the woman who carried food to her dead husband, so Svein rolled behind the mound, sneaked away, and hid behind a memorial stone. From there he could spy on her without being seen.

She approached with a bowl in her hand. From the front he could see her legs but her skirt dragged in the grass behind her. Some keys and other metal objects jingled at her waist. Watching her, Svein momentarily forgot about the king's feast. Two thralls carrying iron-tipped shovels on their shoulders passed behind him. They looked surprised but didn't dare say anything since his clothes indicated that he belonged to the ruling class.

As she exchanged bowls, the woman talked to her husband as she had last autumn. She brushed the scraps and small bones onto the ground, and Svein again felt his body grow tense and hot when her skirt slid to the side and he caught a glimpse high up her thighs. He decided to rape her, just as Geire had raped the smith's wife. But there were too many people around. She might scream and cause trouble. She was, after all, a freewoman and could do as she pleased.

But he noticed a little crevice between this mound and the next one. No one would see them there, and she might not scream anyway. The smith's wife hadn't. All she had done was sob.

No one was around and the woman was sitting on the grave. She thought she was alone so she didn't seem to mind that her skirt fell open and bared her legs. Maybe she liked the cool wind caressing them. The magpies fluttered about restlessly in the nearby birch trees.

Svein could no longer control himself. In a few bounds, he was on top of the woman, grabbing her shoulders, and yanking her to the ground. They tumbled over the edge of the mound and landed in the crevice below. The woman may have been too surprised to scream, or maybe she thought it was her husband. Her eyes were expressionless and she didn't resist when the rapist threw himself on top of her.

But he was too young and too stimulated. He ejaculated before he penetrated her, and after his body had spent itself, he looked up in shame. As if in a dream, he saw two figures with spades over their heads outlined against the sky. Svein crawled away from the woman, who reached feebly after him. He got to his feet and ran off, without looking at the thralls who had witnessed the astonishing interlude played out between the burial mounds.

From the edge of the forest, Svein saw them move on, and a moment later the woman climbed up on the burial mound. She picked up the bowl and looked around before returning to town. Svein was already longing for her, realizing that she hadn't defended herself. Maybe he would have stayed if he hadn't seen the thralls and their spades outlined against the sky. Given a second chance, he probably would have fared better.

Before dusk, Svein saw the boats set out for the king's farmstead, oar blades flashing in the evening sun. He had been turned down as an oarsman and was thinking intensely again about Tora and the king's farmstead. The images kept coming back and all his power had returned. He had just spilled a little of it outside a woman's womb earlier that day.

As he looked out across the still water, he got an idea. He'd go by himself. He didn't have a boat, but there were a few whose owners were far away. He could take one and row to the farmstead. If he waited a while, no one would notice him go ashore, and if it got dark while he was rowing, there'd surely be a fire at the farmstead to guide him.

For a moment he thought about telling his mother but quickly changed his mind. She would either discourage him or insist on coming along. He often tired of her affection for him – and her hatred for others. That night she could just as well sit by herself, go to the sacrificial feast at the temple in town, or be with the Christians opposite the temple, if she wanted.

Small boats were tied up in long rows on both sides of the harbor, and soon he found one he liked. It was trim and almost new. A small boat had just come in, so he waited while the oarsman secured it and disappeared into town.

He rowed past the fortress, watching the small waves splash against the rocks below it. As always, a guard was standing on the rocks, and men's happy voices sounded from inside the guardhouse. The warriors were obviously having a good time. There was a smoldering pile of ashes outside that would be brought to life at sunset as a signal for seafarers. Year after year, it had burned during all of the darkest nights.

The ships from town were almost out of sight now. They were propelled by many oars, and the bows foamed from the speed. They would arrive long before he did, and that was good. Once the festival had started, no one would notice a little boat, rowed by a single man. The island soon lay behind him. Two swans whizzed overhead and landed with a crashing of wings on the water farther away. Some small dark birds in their way took to flight toward the mainland.

The dark, jagged top of a spruce tree was in front of the crest of sun that would soon slip behind the forest. For a moment, Svein hesitated about what he was getting into, but he was stubborn. The girl was his; he had a right to her. He would see to it that no one else took her this wild night when men threw down the first women they could get their hands on.

He could see when the fire flared up and could hear the distant yells when he rested on the oars. He could also see the signal fire at the fortress. His mother was out looking for him right then, he thought spitefully. That would teach her that from now on he was an adult and would go wherever he chose.

A couple of boats left the fishing village on the mainland and headed for the king's farmstead. The people had to be going to the feast. He'd try to land just behind them and follow them to the farmstead. No one would notice him in the dusk.

From the thralls' table, where Holme sat, he heard the king call his name. He got up, wiped his mouth, and walked toward him. Holme had drunk a large tankard of beer with the heavily seasoned meat, and he was happy and in a good mood.

The king was a little drunk, too, and it occurred to him to show off his famous thrall to his guests. He had just told Holme's story and had slightly exaggerated his strength and courage.

Holme was met with shining eyes everywhere as he stood awaiting the king's orders. He still didn't know what was going on and couldn't understand what all these people wanted from him. He didn't see that some of the half-drunk noblewomen were measuring his manly power and weight, while some of the younger men burned to match themselves against him. But he was only a thrall, even if a remarkable one, and they could hardly challenge him.

Holme stood just behind the queen, and she felt permeated by a strange sensation. Ever since the king had emerged from the forest, and the gigantic thrall had had his life in his hands, she had felt in sympathy with him. But this was something else. She wanted to lean backward and snuggle up against him, and she was completely aghast at her desire. Maybe he was a troll capable of attracting anyone he wished.

Still, she couldn't keep herself from turning halfway around to look at him. She saw the massive body, the dark face, calm eyes, and powerful jaw. Again she felt like touching him, and a red flame shot across her cheeks at a forbidden thought. It had to be the mead's fault. She would watch herself and not drink any more.

One of the younger drunken warriors asked the king if he could wrestle with Holme after they had left the table. He would show them how much of the thrall's reputation was based on his boasting and their fear. But the king refused with a laugh, saying he wanted to keep all his warriors in one piece. He'd be needing them in the spring. But the young warrior's eyes flashed with anger, and he didn't relinquish his thought.

The king gestured cordially to Holme to return to his place. Many marveling eyes followed him from the royal table, and still more welcomed him proudly at the thralls' table. He wasn't quite sure what had happened, or what the king had wanted, and he didn't care. He sat down and started in on the meat again. A young thrall woman brought him a full tankard of beer, accompanied by a beautiful smile. Ausi and Tora gave her an angry look as they moved closer to Holme in a gesture of ownership.

Some people had appeared in the meantime and stood near the thralls' table, watching. They were from the fishing village and Svein was with them. No one paid much attention to him, since they thought he was from the farmstead. He stared intently at the table, too, and saw a black head of hair that made a lump form in his throat. But he was relieved to see that Tora was sitting with her parents. He had seen Holme coming back from the king's table, yet he hadn't shuddered as before. Instead he felt a sense of triumph in knowing that no man would dare approach Tora against her father's will.

Before long the king noticed the fishermen with their women and children, and he sent a message to Holme that they should be entertained. Holme got up and walked toward the group, and Svein couldn't help but sneak behind the others. Maybe Holme wouldn't recognize him after all, but he sat down at the far end of the table anyway, hunched over his food as he ate. This was the first time he had eaten with thralls, and his mother would have been furious if she had known. But he didn't feel out of place and even began to enjoy his little adventure. He could keep watch over the smith's daughter all night now. Her eyes and teeth glistened in the firelight, and occasionally she would lean affectionately against her father. Svein liked that somehow.

He drank his beer and got still happier. No one paid any attention to him. He marveled for a moment at the thralls having a table so close to the king's and getting so much food and drink. Those waiting on the king's table would come back now and then to say a few words to their friends. One young thrall looked warmly at another and ran her fingers through his hair before returning to her duties. Observing that, Svein again felt an intense longing. He wasn't contemplating rape anymore, now that he had seen so many warm looks exchanged between men and women at the thralls' table. Now he wanted Tora to come to him of her own free will.

He had no idea how long they had been sitting at the table, but it was completely dark outside the circle of firelight, stars occasionally twinkling through the veil of smoke. At the royal table, the men's conduct was no longer dignified – their beards had become disheveled, their noses were glowing red, and they gesticulated freely when they spoke. The women laughed loudly and frequently and leaned affectionately now and then against whichever man was closest. The fertility god waited rigidly for what would eventually happen. The day's seed had been sown; the night's still remained to be. Beside the wooden god hung the carcass of the pig, white in the firelight. Svein remembered that at the settlement they had always eaten the sacrificial animal after the god had been smeared with blood. But the king had many animals and gave the god the whole sacrifice.

The meal was finally over. The women started cleaning up the tables, then the men moved the tables to one side of the courtyard. The beer tankards and horns stayed where they were; the drinking would continue as long as anyone could lift horn or tankard.

A figure moved into the firelight carrying a large, strange instrument with many horsehair strings on it. In his right hand, the man held something resembling a saw. Svein had never seen anything like this, but he had heard about such things.

About twenty men and women split off from the group surrounding the king and walked in couples into the open yard, the women's arms glowing, supple, and white. The musician steadied the harp against the ground, sat down, and started to play. In short, sonorous notes, he played and replayed the same melody. The dancers began their deliberate movements, passing each other, weaving in and out, and occasionally exchanging partners. All the while, they kept singing the same monotonous song. Many of the observers, who had formed a circle around the dancers, also joined in the singing.

The dance had started slowly, but the tempo gradually increased. Soon it all became a single whirl of bright, laughing faces flashing in and out of view. A skirt would fly out occasionally, revealing an upper thigh; a strange kind of tension started spreading among the observers. They became oblivious to everything else and even the thrall guarding the dead pig was drawn to the spectacle. The dogs were there immediately, leaping at and tearing chunks out of the carcass.

Again and again, the musician played the melody, and now and then Svein caught a word from the song and this made him listen greedily. They sang about what he had seen adults doing when they were lying together, and what he wanted to try again, too. He had failed with the woman on the burial mound that day, but he could probably do better now.

Svein looked around for Tora, finally seeing her flanked by her two parents. Wouldn't she ever be alone? Maybe later, after the dancing stopped. He didn't know what was going to happen, but he felt full of excitement and anticipation. If he didn't get to her himself, he would see that no one else did – if she ever got away from her father and mother, that is. If she wanted to be taken, then he had a right to her.

He saw many of the observers pressing in close to each other and he knew they had singled one another out. The dance went on, more and more passionately. One of the women lost her skirt, or had it ripped off her, but she kept dancing, her smile flashing into view as she whirled past.

The musician finished playing on a grating, harsh, protracted note. The dancers were dripping with sweat, and the observers applauded and cheered their efforts. Svein hoped the dance was over so the rest could begin, but the audience stood still. There was evidently going to be more.

A lot of people, not leaving their places, called for more beer, and three thrall women ran back and forth with tankards. The dancers disappeared into the building, and the woman who had lost her skirt held it in her hand. The men in the audience ogled her lasciviously, but it wasn't yet time.

The king gestured and some men picked up the wooden god and carried him into the circle. He grinned toward the fire, his penis jutting diagonally into the air. The blood that had congealed on him started loosening in the heat, bubbling and hissing softly as it trickled down.

The dancers soon returned in different clothing and gathered around the god. Svein was surprised to see that the men's organs were exposed and the women's skirts, consisting of mere dangling threads or ribbons, reached only to their knees. He saw Holme and other men pulling their young daughters away from the front of the group, and he also noticed the girls only reluctantly letting themselves be led away from the spectacle.

They started dancing in couples again, the tempo building little by little. And again they started chanting. The couples hopped around the god, and after a while the men's organs were erect just like the god's. A murmur of satisfaction passed through the crowd, since everyone interpreted this as a good omen for the next crops.

Svein stood there, mesmerized by the gyrations of the wild dance. The men moved more and more self-consciously as the women became all the more lithe and wild. He noticed several couples break away from the circle of observers and sneak off into the night, unable to restrain themselves any longer. One of the girls pulled away by her father climbed a tree to watch, and her face grew still, a light fleck against the dark tree. Then a child came out of the king's house, its eyes agape. One of the women from the house hurried after the child, picked it up, and carried it back inside.

Holme was alone at the front of the group, and Svein knew that his wife and daughter were somewhere behind him. Although the dance had aroused him and he wanted to see it end, Svein sneaked through the crowd to get closer to the two women. He found them about where he had thought he would. Ausi was standing on tiptoe to see, but Tora stood sullenly behind her, seeming indifferent to everything. That somehow pleased Svein, and he moved closer to try to catch her eye. It was cold there because of all the people standing between him and the fire.

He caught her eye a couple of times, but she must not have recognized him. He had grown a lot since the last time they saw each other. But he was glad she didn't remember him because that might make it a little easier for him to get near her.

The dance either stopped or the dancers did something extraordinary. An impassioned murmur rippled through the circle of observers, and several men broke away with their women and disappeared into the thickets. Single men here and there grabbed women, who sometimes resisted but usually followed apathetically along. A rowdy group of young men came laughing and staggering to where Svein stood, and they grabbed Ausi, Tora, and some other women. Svein tried fiercely to defend Tora, but he was hopelessly outnumbered. He saw her fight a young warrior hard, while her mother made only the feeblest of attempts to free herself. The teeming mass of people, panting and reeking of beer, surged and pressed all around him.

Tora suddenly screamed for her father. There was silence for a moment since many had heard the scream and were waiting to see what would happen. They didn't have to wait long. Holme plowed violently through the crowd, and Svein saw him for an instant. That was the first time Svein was glad for Holme's strength. Then Svein saw Holme clutch the young warrior by the neck in a grip that made the man's arms drop from the girl's chest. He was hurled to one side, landing at the feet of the others.

Tora held her father's hand, looking up at him with a smile of gratitude. At the same time, Ausi's attacker walked past with her toward the bushes. Holme grabbed his arm, and the hand holding Ausi loosened. Then he took Ausi by the hair and dragged her roughly away with him. Everyone made room, and the thralls gathered around to defend Holme if they had to. Soon he was beyond the firelight, and the three of them disappeared toward the smithy.

Svein followed at a distance and was full of joy. His hatred for Holme was gone now, and he felt only admiration. The girl was safe and wouldn't be allowed out again that night. He wouldn't get her, but no one else would either.

Svein also realized that the smith's wife had seemed ready to follow another man into the darkness. He had seen her give up when his uncle Geire had raped her. Holme had been right in grabbing her by the hair. He saw them now silhouetted against the dark sky as they walked on the ridge of the birch-tree hill. Ausi was walking in quiet submission, but Tora was chattering the whole time, her father occasionally grumbling a terse reply.

Svein decided to stay outside the smith's house to see what happened. Maybe Tora would come out alone after her parents had fallen asleep. He could hear the songs and the men's commotion again from the farmstead, but he would rather stay where he was.

After a while, the door opened and Svein quickly hid behind the trunk of a birch tree. Holme came out alone, looked toward the farmstead a moment, and then headed for it. He passed close to where Svein was hiding, and Svein could feel his presence. He wanted to step out and say, 'I've come for Tora.' But he stayed still as the massive figure walked toward the farmstead.

When Holme dragged his wife home by the hair, he had been annoyed by a look he had seen in Ausi's eyes when the other man had pulled her away. It was a look he knew well after many years of living together. Her eyes would halfway close, and she wouldn't blink when she sensed the moment was near. If that young man had slipped away with her in another direction, Ausi wouldn't have been able to resist him.

She was sobbing as Holme built the fire. Tora looked at her angrily and seemed to know what was going on. Ausi's crying annoyed Holme even more. She might be crying because she had missed her chance with the other man.

The thralls had asked Holme to come back; they understood everything. And he ought to go back because they might need his help. The beer made the young warriors boisterous, and they might decide to take a thrall's woman against her and her man's will, if she had any. The king probably wouldn't permit that, but he couldn't be every place at once.

With a few parting words to mother and daughter, Holme walked toward the door. He looked back and met Ausi's eyes. They were filled to overflowing with love and submission, but he left in silence anyway. Maybe she didn't want that other man, after all, he thought, feeling that her eyes followed him through the dark birch grove. She had always been a strange woman. There probably was none better, but she couldn't be trusted at a feast of sacrifice. If someone grabbed her, she would follow along mindlessly. She just couldn't help it.

But she was still young enough to get pregnant, and he didn't want to go through that again. He could still remember a tiny, bluish-white face that had rigidified in the moonlight one frosty night.

Holme hadn't felt any great desire for women during the dance, but then again he had thought that Ausi would come to him after they got home and Tora fell asleep. But Holme's thoughts were busy with women now. The thralls had talked about what could happen that night. One of the thralls had once been sought out by a noblewoman, who had drawn him into the brush. She hadn't been too young, yet even so, the thrall told the story frequently and with pride. He might have just made it up.

All the way there, Holme could hear the commotion from the king's courtyard, and it was all about the same as it had been before. There were a lot of people hopping around laughing and yelling. The thralls welcomed Holme, and a couple of the younger women couldn't conceal their happiness at his coming back alone. They were everywhere he went, and their smiles indicated they were open to anything. But he wasn't experienced with women, and he shyly pushed them aside with a grumble. One of them soon brought him a big tankard of beer and had a look of triumph on her face when he drank it down. He was trying to make himself as happy as his thrall friends.

It was the middle of the night now. A number of people had sneaked off and then returned straightening their clothes; a man or two staggered around with his genitals totally exposed, but no one seemed to mind; and a couple of men started fighting after insulting each other. They crashed noisily to the ground, and the onlookers laughed before dispersing again. The difference between lords and thralls was nearly obliterated as the night wore on and the drunkenness took over.

The king was sitting at his table again, his horn before him. Some of the court women were sitting around him, but they no longer showed him any respect. They were fondling him and laughing and pulling his beard. Each one of them was probably hoping he'd take her when the time was right. There was no sign of the queen, so she might have gone into her house.

Holme was soon feeling the effects of the beer. He was starting to fit in, responding cordially whenever someone talked to him and fondling one of the women, who pretended to stumble and fall against him. He didn't even get angry when the young warrior from before came up to him, wanting to fight. Holme merely avoided him for a while, but the warrior pursued him, challenging him derisively. Holme finally tired of that and noticed, too, that his friends were expecting him to do something. A little ways beyond the firelight, he turned and hurled the warrior on the ground, then walked immediately away. He didn't want an incident at the king's farmstead and was also afraid of really being provoked.

The dazed warrior got up after a while and looked around, and the group of thralls who had witnessed his defeat drew back. He knew now that he never had a chance of beating the smith, since he had found himself on the ground before he knew what happened. But no freeman had been there, so he returned dejectedly to the fire. No one had to know anything about it.

An occasional scream came out of the forest, but not even Holme cared about it now. His women were safe, and the screams could be ones of lust or of distress that night. A lot of the older people started yawning and talking about going to bed. A few of them were already asleep with their heads resting on the table.

Inside the king's house, a woman thrall reported that Holme had returned alone. Several of the court women, who were sitting inside, came to life and went back to the courtyard and feast that they had just left. Again, the queen blushed quickly, and she resentfully watched them go. She had seen their eyes following the king's smith that night and didn't want any of them to have him. She sat there restlessly for a while but soon went out after them, once she had ordered her attendants to stay inside. Darkness had enveloped the high hall once the long fire had been reduced to embers. The queen ran into a man and a woman who affectionately steadied herself against him. For a moment she thought he was the king but walked on, unconcerned. A number of children running around the courtyard were his by other women. But everything was supposed to happen on the bare ground that night. No one was supposed to look for a bed to sow his seed in.

When dawn first appeared like a strip of light in the east, Holme was drunker than he had ever been in his life. He sensed somehow that that was his revenge on Ausi, but he also enjoyed seeing and hearing his thrall friends talking and joking merrily all around him. Everyone wanted to be Holme's friend; they came to him with admiring words about his accomplishments. They knew most about the time he had been master smith in town.

A young woman thrall sat in his lap whispering in his ear. Just as he was about to get up to go with her, he caught an angry and hurt look from a younger thrall. In the midst of his drunkenness, Holme still perceived that the thrall had wanted that woman himself – she just might have been his although the drink had dazed her – and Holme decided, with great effort, to leave her alone. He wasn't going to take anything from a fellow thrall. He was going to stand by them and give them something instead. After he had said a few words to the woman, she got up obediently and approached the other man while those nearby murmured their approval.

But she left a hunger behind in Holme, a hunger that many of the others had already satisfied several times. He got up and started to roam. Many eyes watched him go, but the thrall women didn't think he'd pay any attention to them, so none followed. From the king's house, a figure sneaked off to catch him behind some shrubbery. Another, seeing that, stopped short with an angry grunt.

Holme saw a female form standing before him. Her clothing glittered in the darkness, so he knew she was from the court. He tried to give her room to pass, but she stretched out her hand and stopped him.

He couldn't see her face in the darkness, but he sensed that she was young. She was breathing heavily and said nothing. A ring of keys jingled at her waist when she turned around, indicating that she must be a housewife.

Suddenly Holme understood the situation: she had sought him in the brush to be taken by him. Why else would she be standing there so quietly, breathing so heavily? He was seized by a fierce lust for that free and doubtlessly noble woman. He had never been attracted to anyone except Ausi, but this woman smelled very good. He could imagine how delicate and soft her hands were.

The woman hesitantly reached out to touch him. She was probably trying to encourage him, but he already knew what she wanted and was glad. He took her hand, feeling its smallness and softness, and let his own hand glide up her arm, over and behind her shoulder. Then he put the other behind her legs and lifted her up. She averted her face, but her arms encircled his neck.

He didn't want to stay there in the nearby brush like the others did. Beyond a field rose the black edge of the forest, and he walked toward it. The woman weighed little and was no hindrance. Her keys jingled softly, rhythmically. He vaguely sensed that he was taking his revenge on freemen by carrying one of their women off to the woods. He soon found a dry place, where he laid her down, her face hidden behind one arm. He noticed that she was wearing a knee-length skirt under her long dress, one like those the dancing women had worn. He reached out and moved the keys to one side so they wouldn't do her any harm.

She was much more fragile than Ausi, and that, too, heightened his passion. She groaned and panted under his immense weight, and he twice felt her body tighten, tremble, and then go limp. But he controlled himself, true to the impulse that had made him carry her across the field: he was taking revenge on and insulting the free class through her. He felt like dirtying her face and messing up her clothes and hair so she would look more like a thrall woman.

He felt his power concentrate itself as he fantasized about her delicate limbs, soft hands, and gold-embroidered clothes. He could see a piece of jewelry glimmering at her neck, glowing a soft white in the darkness, and he soon didn't need any help from his imagination, as all conscious thought vanished. The woman stiffened for the third time and stayed that way long after him.

A moment passed before he looked around. Day had broken quickly and he could see all the way to the farmstead, which was almost quiet now. Only some dogs yelping, a bird or two chirping, and occasional voices could be heard. He freed himself, got up, and pulled the clothes over the woman who was still hiding her face. Seeing now that she had to be of the highest rank, he felt an intense sense of triumph, but something else besides. A moment like that would never come again. It had been the noblewoman's whim to take him, but he was a thrall again now. For a moment, he longed for the world of the freemen, to be a powerful man among such women as the one lying on the ground at his feet.

But reality quickly returned. He was a thrall and didn't want to leave thralldom by himself. He had no right to fight for freedom and power just for his own sake.

He heard the woman move and looked down. Without uncovering her face, she motioned for him to leave, motioned with a soft, white hand, a serpentine bracelet wound round her wrist. Holme left, but he followed the edge of the forest around the field rather than walking straight across it. It was so light now that someone might see him otherwise.

He felt very pleased about what had happened. No one would ever find out about it, not even Ausi. He had done what she once had, so it wasn't too easy after all to avoid such things when they seemed destined. He understood that better now.

Some beer was still on the tables and some thralls were still on their feet. A few were asleep on the ground or sat with their heads bowed on their arms. The dogs had torn down the sacrifice, snarling and fighting over it while the early morning magpies chattered in the trees. No one paid any attention. The man guarding the sacrifice had been drunk for a long time and was released from his duty.

A couple of the younger women were still awake, too, but they bore traces of what had befallen them. One of them smiled a smile at Holme that told him she both could and would pay homage to the grinning wooden god again. But Holme had no desire to. The night was over, and he was content. He was also content with how the thralls had been treated during the festivities.

A woman came sneaking out from behind the king's house. She covered her face when she saw people were still in the courtyard. But they didn't pay any attention to her – the same thing had happened only moments before. Only Holme watched her disappear through the door. He would probably see but not recognize her the next day. She could be one of the town women, the wife of one of the most distinguished merchants. Out here, only the queen could have such a large bunch of keys. He took a swallow of the stale beer and headed for home. From a distance, he could see someone by the wall, probably some drunken man trying to lure the mother or daughter out. The person didn't move, and that surprised him. Then he saw that it was a young man, dressed like a freeman, and that one of the windows had been opened.

The young man turned toward him, and there was something strange about the way he moved, something familiar that stirred up dark memories. Holme could see Tora's face in the window, and she looked neither angry nor afraid.

For a moment Holme thought about chasing the young man off, but then he remembered the errand he had just been on himself. It probably wouldn't do too much harm if Tora talked with the boy. She'd be grown soon and didn't often get to see anyone but her parents.

The young man's face was pale in the dawn, yet he walked toward Holme, seeming to prepare himself for anything. He put out his hand with a look that was both respectful and timid. Feeling a greater sense of recognition, Holme took his hand, and Tora smiled. Without a word, Holme continued to the door, which he unlocked with his fancy key.

Ausi greeted him with a mixture of anxiety and tenderness. There were still traces of tears on her cheeks: she had dreaded what Holme might do when he came home and found a young man outside and Tora at the window. Very happy now, she thought only about what might have happened earlier that night. But it was as if she were walking in a dream when she followed the other man who drew her to him.

She had recognized the young man outside but had also seen the great change in him. The hardness and malevolence in his eyes – inherited from his mother – were gone. He was shy, and he talked respectfully to both mother and daughter, even though he was a freeman. And she was not mistaken when she saw how he looked at Tora. He meant them no harm. That was the big change, and it was probably Christ, the god of peace, who had brought it about.

She whispered all this to Holme after they had gone to bed. Tora never left the window, and occasionally she would look back into the darkness with a smile. Strange things were happening, and Holme didn't know what to think. He too had felt that the young man meant them no harm when he offered him his hand. He wouldn't have chanced that if he had had evil intentions. And he wasn't drunk.

Ausi had hoped Tora would fall asleep before Holme did. It was, after all, the night of sacrifice and her body was restless. But Holme was soon sleeping heavily, and she let her thought go. She was still glad, though, that there hadn't been any violence. Holme didn't seem bothered anymore about her weakness earlier that night. But her scalp was still tender where he had grabbed her by the hair and she smiled gently at the thought of it.

Through the open window and smoke vent she could hear a bird singing before she fell asleep. As she drifted off, she heard Tora close the window and go to bed. All was well. She had been anxious about the spring festival but it was over and Holme hadn't fought with anyone. The Christian priests who had recently come to town might have had something to do with that.

Before sleep took her completely, Ausi whispered her thanks to Christ.

Svein eyed the ships in the king's harbor with curiosity as he rowed past them. There was no movement on board and the dragon heads gaped huge and red into the dawn. He noticed some movement on the lookout rocks and shortly after could make out two figures. The watch too had a woman that night. They had something next to them, probably a beer tankard. The woman had obviously brought the guard food and drink. Svein smiled to himself – he didn't begrudge them anything. He had talked with Tora and instead of bridling she had been calm and had even smiled a couple of times. He felt a strong and pleasant certainty that she wasn't going to care about anyone else.

All his bitterness was gone, and he no longer thought of himself as the thrall family's owner. It was hopeless anyway. Holme was alive, and no one could do anything about it. Svein, still feeling Holme's handshake, knew how insignificant he was compared to that man. But Svein was going to be Holme's friend, no matter what his mother might say. He would rebuild the settlement and live there with Tora. And it wouldn't do his mother any good to try to stop him.

The king's fields were newly sown and gray, striped and partitioned by narrow furrows. Beyond them, there was a large burial mound. Holme's house seemed to glide to one side, and it soon disappeared from view. Tora was asleep there. Svein felt his happiness mount again and the power rush into his arms. All thoughts of raping her were gone. He didn't want the trial at the spring assembly, which his mother talked about so often. No one could possibly gain anything by rousing Holme from the peace he was living in. He might leave with his wife and daughter, never to return.

Svein promised himself they wouldn't request a trial. He would get his mother to be quiet about that matter. If she wasn't, he'd have to go his own way and take Holme's side.

The town was asleep when Svein stepped ashore after tying the boat up. A faint smoke hung above the roofs of the houses, growing denser over the heathen temple. He still didn't feel like sleeping, so he walked toward town. Maybe people were still up and about.

He heard voices from the temple. The wooden gods were enveloped by smoke, and people – both men and women – were talking behind them. Their speech was slurred, probably because they were drunk. A gust of wind scattered the smoke, momentarily allowing him a clear view: women and men in various positions, half naked. The spectacle made him stay put until the next breeze came along. He saw even more that time, then walked on, his cheeks burning.

Svein ran into an unfamiliar, thin figure near the Christian church and knew it was one of the newly arrived priests. He got a friendly look but responded to it sullenly, not liking the Christian friendliness that thrived on nothing. Why were they so friendly to people they didn't even know?

His mother was standing in the doorway, her face gray from anxiety and lack of sleep. Svein got angry, his brows knitting together. Was he a little boy who needed tending? He ignored her questions and walked past her into the house. She soon stopped questioning him and put some food out. Something about him told her that from now on, he was a man and would be in charge. She sensed it with bitterness and relief, but above all, she was curious about what he'd been up to that night. She had searched for him everywhere around town, but no one had seen him. Some aging, tipsy men and women had settled down around a fire on the beach. Though poorly dressed, they still had beer and food. Laughing and joking coarsely, they had invited her to join them when she asked if they had seen her son, but she walked on. She had been a chieftain's wife and didn't sit down with just anyone. Besides, her body felt no need at all for a man that night. All such cravings had vanished during her many years of bitterness and vindictiveness.

She was surprised to be hearing Svein himself talking about rebuilding the settlement. They'd take someone from town with them, someone who knew about building, and some thralls who could carry out his orders. The timber was already there. They should start in a few days.

He said nothing when she talked about the spring assembly, but she noticed his face harden. That pleased her since she gave her own interpretation to it. He'd have his revenge on the thrall family, revenge for his stiff neck and everything else. The king himself couldn't save his smith in the assembly. She would have justice at last.

Outside, the morning sun shone on the log walls sealed with mud, on the small, mud-plastered buildings where the twigs and grass stuck through the layer of mud. The town would keep sleeping for a couple of hours, and then life would begin again. Down by the harbor, they were still working on the ship for the raid, and the weapon smithies clanged the whole day. When spring came the hour of the call to arms followed.

Svein's mother had heard about that and was almost glad she didn't have a husband. Svein was still too young and was needed at home to oversee the rebuilding of the settlement besides.

That same day, she was called to the Christians' worship service, and after a moment's hesitation, she went and was baptized. It wouldn't hurt to have the town's chieftain on her side. He helped the Christians but stood against the heathens. Holme was a heathen and there would soon be the spring assembly.

A few days later, a company approached the mainland forest. With the chieftain's help, they had gathered enough thralls to help with the rebuilding and had gotten a horse to haul the lumber. The Christian priest followed them to the harbor and raised his arms above them in a benediction. Svein and the thralls glared at him, but Svein's mother knelt as she had been taught. She had given part of her remaining silver to the Christian church. She hadn't wanted to but had been assured that it would be multiplied for her manyfold. That would come in handy the first few years, before the fields began yielding real harvests.

The chieftain had also promised his help at the assembly if she came to town and made her complaint. The assembly would meet a few days later, and she talked often with Svein about the return journey. He didn't answer, but she saw his face harden every time. His hatred for the thrall family must equal hers, and that pleased her greatly.

Svein worked all day with the others but lived with his mother in the little house Stor and Tan had built in the grove. The day before the assembly, his mother had everything prepared and told him that they'd be back from town in three days and that the thralls should have such and such done by that time. As usual, Svein said nothing. He just walked outside and shut the door. But he had fashioned a piece of lumber to bar the door from the outside. He put it in place, locking his mother inside.

He thought for a moment, then walked to the laboring thralls. He wanted to tell them what was going on so no one would let her out before the assembly was over.

As the thralls listened, grins of satisfaction spread across their faces. They didn't like the woman with the hard face. Nor did they want Holme, who was the thralls' help and refuge, to be brought before the assembly for what he had done for the thralls. They didn't say much, but Svein could tell he had them on his side.

While they were still standing there, the window in the small house banged open.

'Svein!'

The thralls grinned, and Svein pretended not to hear. The screams grew more enraged, more shrill. But the only response they received was the ax blows from the construction work.

After a moment's silence, the woman started yelling again. She turned on the thralls this time, threatening them with the most terrible punishment if they had killed her son or were keeping him from answering her. She commanded them to let her out at once. Still, only the sounds of construction work replied.

It grew quiet again and the next time she yelled, it was in a pitiful voice. Svein waved a pair of thralls up to the house to see what was wrong. The young aspen trees nearby hadn't come into leaf yet, but the buds were swelling and the house would soon be hidden until the leaves fell again in the autumn.

Unobserved, Svein too went to see what was going on and saw that his mother had tried to crawl through the window and had gotten stuck. Her upper body had made it but her middle had expanded in the past few years, so she couldn't push it through or pull it out. The stool had probably toppled over as well, leaving her dangling in the air.

He saw the thralls start pushing her back through the window without saying a word. It was unpleasant to see how they stuffed her breasts over the ledge when they got jammed. It was over quickly, although she hurled insults at them the whole time. They soon returned, smiling at the others, and started working again. Everyone knew that the hard woman was finished, that the son was going to be master of the settlement, and it made them glad.

At midday, the thrall in charge of the food called, and the work stopped. The thralls walked toward where the smoke was rising, their mouths watering as the smell of smoke and grilled meat reached them. They sat on the ground with their wooden bowls and drank water from the spring, which was gurgling constantly on the slope, its water running down over the yellowish chalk deposits.

Svein gazed across the hillside recollecting his childhood, his father, the warriors, and the thralls, the rock that came hurling from the forest to make his neck rigid for all time. But his thoughts sped past Holme without rancor, stopping at Tora. The house had to be big and roomy, so she would feel at home. She was a thrall's daughter, but Holme was no normal thrall. He was somehow superior to everyone. It wasn't easy to explain.

When Svein looked out over the cove, he remembered his mother's plaintive cry for him as the invaders dragged her away. And then he looked toward the little house, now completely quiet. He sent a thrall with a bowl of food, a piece of bread, and a tankard of water for his mother. The provisions had to be passed in through the window. The door had to stay shut until the assembly was over.

The new building rose like a huge barn from the slope, only its roof missing. A couple of thralls had laid the clay floor and leveled it with their wooden spades. It had dried fast, but here and there you could see pieces of straw sticking up through the cracks where it was still drying. The hearth in the middle of the hall was lined with stones for the long fire. Holme's old smithy in the rocks was being put to use again, and a thrall who knew something about smithing was making links, hooks, and tripods for the caldrons.

The thrall felt the bowl of food and tankard of water being taken from his hand, and then he heard the threats repeated. If they had harmed her son, they'd all die. But if he'd open the door and let her out, he'd be granted his life and a reward to boot.

Only the wind, moving through the young aspens, answered her. She thought about the spring assembly, which would meet the next day, but she wouldn't be there. Once again, Holme, his wife, and daughter would slip through her fingers.

She started thinking about Christ, whispering promises of great gifts for Him if He'd only help her escape. But as she did so, the image of the charred black god on the stone came to mind, and so she promised him a sacrifice in turn. Maybe things would have turned out differently if she had given him something to begin with. She had seen him still standing there on the stone when they had come out of the forest but thought he couldn't help her. After all, he had witnessed the settlement burning and her being captured without doing anything. Nevertheless, he was still there when everything else was gone. Maybe he did have some power. He was still the household god of her husband and his father.

She didn't know that at that moment, Svein was placing meat and bread before the god as the thralls mumbled their approval. The work had gone well, they felt happy, and it must be because of the god. He had survived a great deal but had stayed at the settlement, and that awakened their respect and reverence.

Svein's mother had put the food on the floor, with no intention of eating it. But the fragrance of cooked meat and roots filled the air, and she hadn't eaten since the night before. If the thralls had killed Svein, they surely would have killed her at the same time. That would have been the easiest thing to do. But here they were giving her food, obviously wanting her to live. That had to mean that Svein was alive, too. Then what was going on? She put the thought aside for a while as she started eating. There was still a battle to be fought. She wanted to fight it, and so she had to eat the thralls' food to have the strength. Besides, she felt in her heart that Svein was still alive; perhaps he had just been taken prisoner so the thralls could live at the settlement by themselves.

All this while the first free thrall who had fought by Holme's side lived at the other farmstead. He had labored both day and night and had managed with the help of an old man to keep up both house and field. No one had objected, so he started thinking of the farmstead as his own. The old man had shown up begging and had been allowed to stay; he was good at mending nets and hunting up food.

One day while he was still holding his mother prisoner, Svein felt like taking a walk to the other farmstead. There probably wasn't much left of it, but he wanted to walk where he had walked as a child and see where his forefathers had settled. He remembered the day the pirates from the east burned both farmsteads and took his mother captive. Only his uncle Geire and he were alive then to seek revenge, and now Geire lay in one of the town's countless burial mounds. Holme had killed the powerful warrior with his bare hands. But Svein, of his own accord, had recently offered his hand to the killer, the man he had once hated, and he had felt death in Holme's grip. He felt neither hate nor terror any longer – he knew somehow that there was a way to be friends with the fearful man. You could walk right up to him without danger if you had good intentions in your heart.

Svein noticed how much the forest had grown during the past few years. The path vanished for long stretches, probably because the cattle weren't walking in the forest anymore. But their mooing would soon be heard again in the area, and they would come down to the settlement for milking just like they did during his father's day. Men and women thralls would be there. And – this last thought stuck in Svein's chest – Tora would come as the mistress of the house. He would convince her parents how good it would be for her. His mother's hatred for the smith's family also came to mind, but he'd keep a tight rein on her. She wasn't going to decide anything.

Svein's head swarmed with plans for the future, so his walk passed quickly. He was soon at the edge of the forest looking toward the farmstead. There was only one little building left, the one the fire had spared, but it didn't look as dilapidated as he had expected. No one was in sight, but he had the feeling that someone was nearby. A little boat lay at the shore, and the jetty bore traces of having been recently repaired. Maybe some distant relative had come and taken over the farmstead. Or maybe some outlaw had dared stay there for a while.

No matter what, though, the farmstead belonged to Svein and his mother. No one had a right to settle there without permission. Then he saw various farming implements – spades and plows. And the field had been sown, the new green crop carpeting the ground. But where were the people? He'd find them and tell them who owned the farmstead.

But before he had time to take a step, a muffled, twanging sound came from some bushes in front of the little building. He felt a cold puff of wind on his cheek, and when he looked around, saw an arrow quivering in a tree trunk a few feet away. It had been meant for him. He started running back on the path, not knowing how many or how dangerous his enemies might be.

After he had disappeared, the free thrall got up and looked in the direction he had gone. He didn't know who the visitor was, but he had a feeling he was an unwelcome guest. It was just as well to greet him in a way he couldn't misunderstand. The thrall had worked day and night and was determined to defend what he had accomplished.

His woman came out and put their baby down on the ground. The child crawled to his father and reached for the bow, and then the thrall hurried them back into the building. He suspected that the young man at the edge of the forest was a spy and that at any moment, he'd have to contend with other foes, more of them and more dangerous. After a while, he walked to the edge of the forest and pulled the arrow out of the tree. It had a good point and he could use it.

He was uneasy all day long, walking around, listening and watching, too worried to work. The old man was fishing outside the belt of reeds and would glance at him occasionally with a look of surprise on his face.

For the first time the free thrall was thinking about how secure he'd feel if Holme were around. Together, it was easy to fight and defend themselves, but, alone, it was hard to know what to do. And they had vowed to help each other. But Holme lived at the king's farmstead and couldn't know if any enemies came out of the forest and killed the thrall and his family.

The thrall whittled shafts for all of his arrowheads, and he gathered a pile of stones as big as his fist to throw. He sharpened his axes with a whetstone. All the while, he knew he could expect no mercy if it was freemen who were out after him. But whether Holme was alive or dead, the thrall was honor bound to fight and kill as many free men as possible before it was his turn to fall.

The day passed without event. It might have been a forest troll that had taken a young man's form at the edge of the forest. The thrall had seen and heard strange things before. Maybe he would have another year of peace to enjoy the farmstead as his own.

He was awake until midnight, and his last thought was to find Holme to get his advice. He was the one free thrall, and Holme was his friend. He would advise him and help him as he had done before.

He woke a few hours later, glad to see that nothing had changed. Beside him lay his wife and child, and the old man slept in the corner, his toothless mouth gaping in his beard. The singing of birds and an occasional seagull's cry from the cove floated through the smoke vent. When he cautiously peered out the door, he saw the lake glittering in the morning sunlight. Maybe the young man from the day before had been alone and had happened by accidentally.

But his old calm wouldn't return, and he decided that in the afternoon he would go to the old deserted settlement where Holme had once been a smith. If everything was as it ought to be there, he could relax. Only from there could danger threaten. The old chieftain's repulsive witch of a wife and her son were the only ones who had a right to either farmstead.

Even at a distance, he could hear the blows of hammers and axes. Like Holme many times before, he sneaked toward the edge of the forest and peered out. He saw an unfinished, rather large, new building, and several men working on it. He also saw the young man he had shot an arrow at the day before. And he understood immediately who he was and what was going on right in front of his eyes. The mother and son were rebuilding the old settlement.

Tears of sorrow and rage ran down the thrall's cheeks. His freedom would soon end, and he would get nothing for all the work he had done. All he could expect was to be run down and killed. There would surely be no mercy shown for some thrall who had dared live as a freeman on his own farmstead.

He stood there watching the work for a long time. The new building wasn't where the old one had been but a little farther away instead. The old place was probably full of bad luck. He wished again that Holme were with him. Together they could attack and drive off or kill the trespassers. But alone he was powerless to stop the workers, who had axes and other weapons within reach.

As he walked back, the thrall knew there was only one thing for him to do: he had to hide his family and go to Holme at the king's farmstead. But he might be able to take his family with him.

Holme had done that more than once when he was being hunted by the freemen.

On the afternoon of the last day of the assembly, Svein's mother heard the bar being drawn from the door. She waited a while, but it didn't open. She was furious but afraid at the same time of what she would see outside. She had heard the work going on the whole time and had gotten a bowl of food regularly. Why were they keeping her alive if they had killed Svein?

Finally, she pushed the door open and peered out. No one was outside threatening her. The leaves had grown bigger while she had been locked up and were obscuring the surroundings.

She sneaked anxiously through the bushes and saw the new building. The work was going on as usual, and the lumber worker was giving his instructions. The roofing had begun, and the building would be finished in a few days. But would she be allowed to live there? And where was Svein?

After a while she heard wheels squeaking, and she soon caught a glimpse of the horse's back at the edge of the forest. A thrall was driving a large load for the roof. Svein walking beside him with a spade. He looked all right, and she was deliriously happy that he was still alive. Why had he let them shut her up during those crucial days? She had yelled repeatedly through the window that she had to be at the assembly.

Svein saw her come fluttering out of the foliage and rushing toward him, and he exchanged a knowing look with the thralls. He had asked them to let her out while he was in the woods.

No one responded to her as she raged, questioned, and threatened. In the end, she sank exhausted onto a log, and then Svein spoke. He said that it had all been for the best. Everyone who had fought against or pursued Holme had lost in one way or another while he always helped his friends. From now on, Svein wanted to be friends with Holme. He was a thrall, but an extraordinary one. The king treated him better than he did his warriors.

The men around him listened while they worked more quietly, and the lumber worker nodded, as if to his stick, as he was measuring. Svein's mother berated her son, calling him a thrall and a coward, but he didn't respond, and she felt that nothing would give her words any power. They kept working, talking among themselves, not paying any more attention to her than if she had been a crow cawing or a pig grunting. But she wasn't finished yet. She would go to town and complain to the Christian chieftain. To add to his other crimes, Holme had corrupted Svein with his witchcraft. Something must have happened at the spring festival when she was looking for him all night.

She would rest a few days before going to town. Maybe the witchcraft would wear off by then, and Svein would be himself again. Just a few days ago, she had seen his face harden with loathing when she described what she would do to Holme's wife and daughter, once she got hold of them. But Holme was still alive, and not even the chieftain seemed able to cope with him.

She'd still complain to him one more time, though. Svein was walking around like a thrall among thralls and that couldn't be allowed for long. That he seemed happy doing so just showed how powerful the witchcraft was. Maybe Christ could set him free. She had heard He could do such things better than any god before Him.

When she walked past the charred wooden god on the stone, she noticed that some meat had been placed before him. Svein or the thralls had put it there, and the god had also shown that he was on their side. But he could have helped her instead; she'd offered him sacrifices ever since she was a child. Furious, she picked up the piece of meat and hurled it down the hillside, the flies buzzing around her hands.

All day long, she kept a sulky distance from the men and didn't respond when Svein yelled for her to fix some food. They fixed their own food while they held her prisoner, so they could now too. She saw one of the older men set his ax aside and walk to the hearth, still smoking with hot ashes. She went to bed hungry, but after everyone was asleep, she got up and scavenged around in the twilight of the spring night until she found something to eat.

Because she kept away from the building again the next day, she couldn't hear what a rider from the forest had to say. He was very excited, and all of them crowded around him. Svein turned red in the face and looked around in perplexity, and his mother felt at once uneasy and curious. The man soon rode on, and the work gradually started up again. But Svein often rested on his tool, looking either toward where the man had disappeared or out over the cove.

That evening, she managed to learn that the stranger carried the call to arms. For a moment, she worried that Svein might have to represent the farmstead in battle. But he was too young, and there was no master here. He had to stay home this time.

Svein was uneasy the whole day, not knowing what he wanted to do. He imagined the big fleet with its beautiful sails furled and the golden-red maws of its dragon heads pointing toward foreign lands, where there would be gold and silver to plunder. But he could see Tora, too, and the building; if he left, it would have to take care of itself. The settlement should be put in order first, with Tora as mistress; then would be the time for him to go raiding.

His mother grew uneasy, too, when she heard that the call had gone out. The king and the chieftain would soon set sail, and then who would ensure her justice? She would have to leave the next morning before Svein and the thralls woke up. She told herself with disgust that since Svein had become friends with the thralls, she didn't have to worry about leaving him alone with them.

The free thrall didn't dare go to the ferry station, so he walked instead to where they had landed after escaping from the fortress. Several small boats were always there, and in the forest above lived their owners in little mud huts. He got there with the first light of day, and no one was awake. He was going to borrow one of the boats for the day. He ought to be back before nightfall, and the owner could have his boat back again.

He knew that old people were living there, and so he wasn't afraid. When it became completely quiet for a moment, he went down and untied the best boat. But he heard scurrying steps and some panting on the path he'd just left. He quickly untied the knotted rope in an effort to row out and away, but couldn't finish before a woman came down the path. She couldn't know that the boat didn't belong to him, so he calmed down again.

It was a middle-aged woman, and he could tell from her voice when she asked for a ride that she belonged to the free class. He wanted to chase her off, but if she raised a fuss, the boat's owner might wake up. He signaled for her to step into the boat and then shoved off.

For a moment, he heard a peculiar buzzing sound from town and couldn't figure out what it was. He had taken the boat into a cove and so had to row a good while before the town came into view. The buzzing intensified and the woman stared toward the town with uneasiness and rage. It might have been foolish to have taken her along; it would have been better had he rowed along the skirt of reeds alone until he was farther away.

The woman ordered him to row faster and he obeyed. He

could tell she was used to giving orders, and he forgot for a moment that he was free. He would put her ashore a ways from town and then move on.

When they got outside the point hiding the town from view, he heard the woman cry out in dismay; he turned around. He rested on his oars in total astonishment, staring at the overwhelming sight. Sail upon sail obscured the entire island, and the dragons glistened powerfully in the rising sun. A fresh morning wind had just come up and was met with great jubilation from the ships. It was a good sign. Smoke rose from countless sacrifices in the town, and a burned smell filled the air.

He coasted on his oars, looking with constant pleasure at the long row of ships. Meanwhile, he gave half an ear to an angry stream of words from the woman in the stern. She was always late, people treated her poorly. Then he heard her let go scornful, hard words about someone, a black-haired thrall smith, a man who should have been killed a long time ago. He had done her more harm than anyone else.

The free thrall listened intently now, scrutinizing her closely. She kept telling her woeful story without even glancing at him. As she watched the ships, she said she should have come the day before. Another summer would pass by now without her getting her due.

The thrall rowed on, but with a new expression in his eyes, a watchful, sly expression. He had begun putting things together. The woman had come from the direction of the settlement, hated Holme, and talked about a son. She said she might as well go back since the king and the chieftain were both gone. But she decided to go to town and see to her house.

The woman watched the fleet of Viking ships so intently that she didn't notice the thrall changing course when he started rowing again. He headed for the woods northwest of the fortress, his thoughts racing. What would be the best thing to do? The best thing would be if the farmstead's owner were dead. That would leave only the son, and there would always be some way out with him.

His face had taken on a hard and crafty expression, but he looked down when the woman turned to castigate him for not heading toward town; he answered sullenly that he wouldn't go there. She was free to go wherever she wanted on foot.

Before he knew what to do, the boat neared the shore where the rocks jutting out below the fortress blocked the town from view. The woman was still watching the ships intently when he stopped rowing, pointed an oar at her chest, and gave a sharp shove. She tumbled into the water with a scream, and he rowed quickly away. Into the belt of reeds, so no one would see the boat. He heard screams and splashing for a moment, and then excited voices on the shore by the fortress. He rowed with powerful strokes and soon had the whistling reeds enveloping him. The woman's birch-bark basket was still in the boat and he regarded it hopefully. He'd risk stopping after a while to look inside. His food was gone, and he hoped there was some in the basket.

After following the belt of reeds for a while, he chanced rowing into the open water. He would put ashore a long way from the king's farmstead and approach through the woods. The forest afforded him safety, but out on the lake he was visible and exposed. But the king was away now with most of his men so it was less dangerous than usual.

A thought made his face darken, and he rested on his oars. The king might have taken Holme on the raid, one man who was worth several when it came to fighting or working. That depressed him, but he kept going anyway. If Holme hadn't wanted to follow along, no one could have forced him.

It was quiet after the ships had disappeared. He didn't hear a sound from the shore or from the king's farmstead. There wasn't a boat in sight, large or small. He grabbed the woman's basket, opened it, and ate the meat and bread as the boat drifted slowly with the waves. He looked around as he chewed, and when he had finished eating, he drank some lake water with the little wooden ladle that was tied to the basket with a thong.

While eating the woman's food, the free thrall felt glad about what had just happened. Even if Holme had gone with the king, he still might be able to get by and guard his farmstead. Thralls were rebuilding the other one; they would surely have no objection if their new master disappeared. An arrow could reach him from the edge of the woods or a spear come flying if he happened onto the forest path alone again. And while the warriors were away, there could be no retribution against the thralls.

Revivified, he began rowing again and soon approached the woods where he would land. He saw the fishing village across from the king's farmstead in the distance, but he saw no movement there. Some of its strongest men were probably with the king. On such a raid, they needed men who knew something about everything: smiths and other craftsmen, fishermen and hunters who could find food for the troop.

He was soon stepping ashore near where Holme had once stepped. He hid the boat and started walking toward the king's farmstead, not even bothering to move stealthily or be on guard. It was so quiet and peaceful here. No enemies, nothing to fear. And he'd soon find out whether or not Holme was at home.

At the spring assembly, the chieftain looked around in vain for Svein and his mother and was relieved at their absence. The day the king had designated for the raid was approaching, and a lot remained to be done. That stubborn woman would only have caused him trouble.

Since the new priests had arrived, the number of Christians had increased and kept growing every day. The church still stood on the piece of land he had donated, and the rich woman's gifts of silver and gold glistened on the altar. The king would issue a strict order that the Christians had the right to spread the Word freely and peacefully while the Vikings were away. And without a leader, the heathens wouldn't dare disturb or injure them. The thrall smith was in the king's service and wouldn't again begin his foolish struggle to turn the thralls into freemen.

The chieftain looked with disgust at the sacrificial smoke rising for the journey and heard the heathen priests invoking their gods. The Christians stood in a silent group, doubtlessly hoping in their hearts that the enterprise would fail and the heathens would be cut down by enemies in the foreign land. As for himself, the chieftain was sure he'd return safely. The Christian priest had assured him of that and the casting of lots had indicated it, too.

When the ships were rowed up toward the wind, the heathen priests' shouts swelled into wild screams. The women waved, some of them weeping as they stretched their arms out to their husbands on the ships. Those standing closest to the king's ship heard him promise the battle god great sacrifices if he would grant their mission success. Then the king looked around at the mainland and the islands and promised sacrifices to the fertility god if he saw to it that the year's harvest was good and plentiful.

Once the fleet was out of sight, the people left behind returned to their dwellings. Many women were still crying, and the town was oppressively quiet and empty. The watch stood on the rocks as usual, and outside the fortress lived those warriors who had stayed home to defend the town. The slope was fortified with rocks and ramparts in several places.

The watch and the warriors hadn't noticed the thrall and the woman in the small boat that could be seen momentarily beyond the rocks. But they heard screams and splashing, and a couple of them ran down to the shore on the other side of the rocks. The reeds were dense from the shore outward a couple of boat lengths, but there was a path cut through the reeds and a little boat nearby. The men rowed it out quickly and saw something sputter, gurgle, and sink. Just below the surface of the water, they could see a woman's clothes, so they grabbed hold, pulled the woman's head above the water, and towed her to shore behind the boat.

She lay for a moment snorting and hiccuping, the water streaming off her, and she looked wild and terrible with her dripping wet hair hanging over her hard face. The men were seized by fear. Where had she come from? There wasn't a boat in sight, and no one could have gotten into the water from land. They looked at each other and read each other's minds. It had to be a lake troll they had dragged up. They beat a hasty retreat, clambering hand and foot up the slope. From the top, they looked back, panting. The troll was sitting upright now, trying to get the hair out of its face. It was mumbling and hissing. The men realized they should have thrown it back into the lake, but they didn't dare get close a second time.

A little while later, all the men were standing on the hilltop, weapons in hand, looking silently at the creature on the shore. She was still fussing with her hair but had hung her garment on a bush to dry. She looked more like a normal woman now in her short jacket and bare legs. But where had she come from? The two who had dragged her up assured the others in a whisper that she had popped straight up out of the water. Maybe she'd go back where she came from soon.

The men stood there for a long time, and more and more joined them. Finally they saw the creature take its garment from the bush and feel it. It wasn't dripping any more, and she had tied her hair in a knot. After a while, she glanced up at the group of men, then began climbing toward them. They looked at each other and began pushing each other back to the fortress. The creature walked right through it and out the gate that connected to the town, the gate through which people fled into the fortress when danger threatened. The men breathed a sigh of relief and gradually returned to what they had been doing. They didn't talk about what had happened until just before nightfall.

Despite their austere silence, the Christian priests watched with inner jubilation as the sails of the heathen fleet retreated and disappeared behind the islands and islets. Their work would be easier now that the number of heathens wasn't so many times as great as their own. The most powerful and most dangerous were gone. It was probably God's will that these stubborn people of the north should finally be baptized.

The Christian chieftain was gone, too, but they had come to an agreement with him about how things should go. The rich woman gave them all the coins and silver they needed. She felt sick and asked them to pray for her soul day and night. And she paid with the silver her husband had pirated on the high seas and in distant lands. The Christian priests were constantly in attendance upon her, and their God, who didn't accept sacrifices, never seemed to get enough gifts.

In their homeland, the priests had heard a lot about the Swedes who didn't want to emerge from their heathen darkness and worship Christ. They clung tenaciously and austerely to the gods of their fathers, and hell didn't terrify them. Only great need and their own gods' disfavor could make them, for a short time, turn to Christ and pray for His help. But when the danger was past, sacrificial fires were soon burning again in the heathen temples and shrines. There must be a reason for all this. It wasn't the king, who had kindly given them permission to preach freely. But the king didn't have a great deal of power in this curious land where even the thralls were defiant enough to pitch themselves against their earthly masters.

The town was empty and quiet now. God's word should be victorious this summer. When the warriors returned, if God let them, their wives and daughters would be baptized members of the Christian congregation. Many of the men should then follow suit and the victory would be won.

The two priests talked with the rich woman about that. They also learned the story about the thrall smith, the Christians' deadliest enemy. They heard about the uprising he had led against their predecessors and about his distributing their grain among the starving thralls. The woman thought the smith was the greatest obstacle in Christ's path. If it wasn't for him, the thralls would come to Christ in droves.

The priests listened and then told about an adversary of Christ's, named Saul, who had once turned into a great man of God. That could even happen with the smith. But the woman shook her head and said that they didn't know him. And they ought to keep their distance. The priests answered as their predecessors had always done, however, that their lives lay in God's hand. Then they walked out of the rich woman's house with dignity, carrying new gifts to their church.

They saw a strange creature coming along the fortified road leading to the fortress – a woman with wet hair wrapped on top of her head and dressed in wet, wrinkled clothes. She had an angry, threatening expression on her face. Since the priests considered it their duty to alleviate all that was painful and hard, they stopped the woman and gently inquired, in their broken Scandinavian, what was troubling her. They knew someone who could help in all times of need and for nothing. And they gazed kindly at her, their gifts in their hands.

Svein's mother stared back at them, her hard eyes flashing as the old thoughts returned. Everyone had deceived her; no one had helped her get revenge and justice. Maybe the Christians would.

So she followed the new priests toward the church while she repeated the story of Holme once more. As the rich woman had done, this strange creature insisted that as long as the smith was alive, the Christians would be talking in vain about their God. Holme was a great sorcerer, and the king protected him in spite of all his crimes. Therefore, he should be done away with while the king was away, and his family should be returned to her, their rightful owner.

The priests heard the woman out, then walked pensively into the church after inviting her to the evening's worship service. In a short space of time now, two women had pointed out what prevented the kingdom of Christ from expanding in this part of Scandinavia. It might be their duty to strike that barrier down. Everything seemed to say so. The king and his warriors had sailed off to the east; the smith had many enemies. The time was surely at hand to dispose of him. This black-haired man of violence was clearly no new Saul whom Christ would strike with blindness to make a Paul of him.

As their predecessors in town had often done, the priests prayed for some sign and guidance from Christ. And they soon felt the answer in their hearts. It was they who should dispose of God's enemy. How they did it didn't matter.

Fortified by the Spirit, they counted yet again the gifts of gold, coins, and silver rods the rich woman had given them in exchange for their praying for her. She was sick now and anxious, despite everything, that the devil would take up the struggle for her soul. She still had bountiful wealth. Her daughter, having been baptized too, humbly submitted when the priests told her how impossible it was for a rich person to enter into heaven. She hadn't laid claim to her earthly inheritance once she had understood that what those gentle-eyed men were taking from her was only a hindrance to a blessed life.

And they soon got corroboration that they were on the right track. The rich woman took a turn for the worse and became yet more anxious about her soul. She still had considerable wealth. To be assured of happiness, she wanted to do even more. She had heard that you should also give to the poor, but there weren't many poor people in town. Most people were well off and owned many thralls. She didn't think about the many homeless, oppressed people who lived off the land with no roof over their heads. They were mere thralls, and their poverty was God's just punishment. Neither did she think about setting her own or anyone else's thralls free or about giving them any other aid.[9]

When the priests thought they couldn't accept more from the woman, they advised her to send gifts to a town in the south where a number of poor Christians lived.[10] The priests there would accept the gifts and divide them among the most needy. The woman perceived immediately that Christ was speaking through them, so

9. Rimbert essentially tells the same story of the wealthy woman, Frideburg, and her daughter in chapter 20 of the *Vita Anskarii* (*Anskar*, pp. 70–73). The hermit Ardgar was in charge of the mission in Birka at this time. See note 6, p. 61.

10. The town is Dorstadt (*Anskar*, p. 72).

she called her daughter and ordered her to go to the Christian town with the gifts.

A few days later, the starving, homeless thralls from the town and its environs saw the daughter with an attendant, carrying a heavy sack of silver coins, step aboard a ship that would sail to the town where poor Christians lived. Two gray-clad figures, a short one and a tall one, raised their hands over her in a blessing. The thralls stared at the departing ship, still not comprehending what was going on and unaware that they lived in a town without poverty.

After the priests had seen the ship disappear, followed by their blessings, they returned to the church, their minds on their other God-ordained duty: to dispose of the man who, above all others, blocked their path. They had to proceed judiciously; there were still masses of heathens whom it wasn't wise to provoke. They could still marshal a force and run their wooden gods' bloody errands. Somewhere among the thousands of burial mounds lay one of their predecessors, a Christian priest the heathens had killed. He was awaiting redress now on the great Day of Judgment when, in pious jubilation, he would get to see the heathens burning in hell.

From the altar in the dark recess at the front of the church glittered some of the rich woman's gifts; others lay in an iron-bound box. A Christian thrall stood watch day and night. He received no earthly compensation for his faithfulness, simple-mindedly waiting instead for what the priests had promised him beyond the portion of ground that would one day be his. But whenever he passed the heathen temple, he scurried by without responding to the abusive words the temple attendants hurled after him. He wasn't so sure yet that the wooden gods were as harmless as the Christian priests made them out to be.

After the rich woman had given away all the treasures her husband had stolen, she died with her eyes anxiously fixed on the silver cross in the priest's hands. Only a rumor of her generosity passed among the starving and homeless in the town and surrounding area. The heathen priests didn't get so much as a goat to sacrifice to their gods. Their eyes shot daggers at the Christian priests who passed with dignity, and they frequently asked their gods to destroy them to show everyone their power. They also took council with the merchants, who were still faithful servants of the gods, over the best way to hurt the Christians while the king and his army were away.

A dark figure occasionally passed through their minds, and they wished he were still in town. The Christians' old enemy, who had destroyed their temple and stolen their grain during the famine – he was the one who knew best how to handle them. The Christians were under the king's protection, but if the heathens could provoke his smith against them, nothing could dissuade Holme.

For now, though, the Christian priests had the upper hand. They walked around among the lonely women, who lived in constant fear for their husbands, telling them that Christ alone could bring their husbands back to them alive. And even if the men fell in foreign lands, the couples could still be reunited after death. Many pining women couldn't resist that thought, and the Christian church was soon filled for every worship service. The gifts streamed in, and coffers filled with silver and gold were sent by ship to the mother church in the priests' home parish.

The wooden gods glared threateningly out over their shrinking throngs of worshipers and diminishing sacrifices. Their priests prophesied destruction of a land and people who fell away from the gods that had granted them and their fathers good fortune and success, hoping in their hearts for misfortunes that could be blamed on Christ and his priests. Then the showdown wouldn't be far away. There might be as many Christians as heathens in town, but they were mainly women, unable to fight. They'd undoubtedly return to the wooden gods anyway if something happened to their husbands.

And so the hostility grew quietly during the warm, clear days of early summer. The Christians grew more confident, and one day both priests walked through town carrying some object in front of them. Behind them walked a group of women and a couple of older men, two by two. They sang protractedly, staring solemnly ahead. The heathen priests stood in the hall of their temple, laughing loudly and scornfully as the crowd passed by. The rich woman's daughter had returned, and it was rumored among the Christians that Christ had sent back the silver she had given out for His sake. She was much esteemed for that and followed right behind the priests.

Svein's mother was with the women. The priests had promised her that within a short time, Christ would destroy her black-haired enemy and return his wife and daughter to her. She didn't want to return to the farmstead before she had seen a little of that, but she waited impatiently. Her old dream took on new life. Her son and everyone else would see her come back with Ausi and Tora once Holme had been killed. It had to be that way in the end. Never before had a thrall family been allowed to live after so much defiance and so many crimes.

With that hope in her heart, she promised gifts to Christ, adding threateningly that it all had to happen quickly. She'd waited long enough. And no one knew when the king would return with the army. A message had come from the east, so everyone on the island knew that the voyage had gone well thus far. And so there were worship services in both temples again. There was mournful singing in one, loud laughter and drunken gaiety in the other. One glittered with gold and silver; the other witnessed animal carcasses roasting, blood running down the statues of the gods. Both took credit for the safe arrival of the Viking fleet at its destination.

The king stood in the smithy thinking for a long time. It might be a good idea to take the powerful smith along on the raid; he was experienced and could give sound advice. But the warriors would get upset and derisive if he took advice from a thrall in such important matters. And Holme was too good to take along only as a smith. His rightful place was at the head of the warriors, but that could never be.

They'd also need a man at home who could take responsibility for everything on the farmstead. Hostile ships could show up while they were away, and someone had to be there who could decide whether to fight or run. The queen and her companions had to be protected, and no one could do that better than Holme. He could help the foreman with the work in the fields and meadows. The thralls looked up to him and would do what he asked without complaint.

Men were working eagerly on the king's ship in the harbor, and far away near the town on the island, you could see a line of colors. It was the sails of the dragon ships that had arrived and were now waiting for the departure. They would sail early the next morning if there was a good wind. The king had directed that sacrifices be made both at the farmstead and in town to the weather spirits.

From the smithy the king could see parts of his fields, where the sprouts rose level and green. The foreman was a skillful farmer, but he knew nothing about fighting and defending himself. It was probably best to leave the smith behind. Holme and the other men left at home would form the queen's guard.

Holme looked at the king in silence, but a glimmer of satisfaction came into his eyes. He had wondered what would happen and felt no desire to travel to a distant land. He had never enjoyed fighting, although he had often been forced into it by his enemies. He tried to imagine what it would be like to fight people in the other town, but only felt uneasy. They had never seen him before and couldn't have done him any harm, so why should he fight and maybe kill many of them?

But now the king was telling Holme that he would stay behind to protect those still at the farmstead. The thralls could help him; they were strong men and did what he told them. And he knew what to do if the farmstead were attacked. But it was better to flee if the odds were against him. The king also said that he felt more confident putting the queen under Holme's protection than he would under anyone else's in the kingdom.

Holme said little in response, but the king knew him well. He had tested Holme many times and was no friend of words himself. A man was someone who acted instead of talked. The king said something more about weapons that should be forged while he was away. Many men would undoubtedly lose theirs in battle.

Early the next morning, all the people of the farmstead had gathered at the harbor, from the king's closest followers to the thralls who hadn't yet begun work. They formed a separate group a little ways away. The sacrificial smoke was still rising from the temples and was blown toward the harbor, which everyone interpreted as a good omen. The night had been calm, but a breeze started across the lake with the rising sun, making dark ripples on the water. It moved across the land and passed on over the swaying treetops. The queen and some of the warriors' wives boarded the ship to accompany their husbands to town.

Holme hadn't gone with Ausi and Tora to the harbor; he

watched the departure from the smithy instead. A vague longing gripped him as he watched the sails and the water. But he hadn't been at the farmstead for long, and a thrall should stay home to work when freemen ventured out in the world. He probably still could have gone with them, but he didn't want to abandon Ausi and Tora. There was also a voice within him, one he didn't quite understand, that said he'd be needed at home. He had heard it before and knew it always had some meaning. Freemen had the spirits of relatives, who showed themselves or whispered advice into their ears when danger was near. It was possible that he too had such a spirit, even though he was a mere thrall.

In any case, he should do what the king requested of him. The king was the best master in the land, but no one followed his example; they just kept on whipping their thralls, killing them, and abandoning thrall babies in the woods. The king was powerless to stop that, even if he tried. He was the supreme commander in battle, and the one who ruled over the kingdom's great festival of sacrifice, but otherwise his power was no greater than the leading chieftain's.

Holme felt the old sting in his chest when he thought about the thralls' misery. Here, where they were treated almost like freemen, it would be so easy to forget about what was happening on other farmsteads and in town. But he couldn't do that. At the moment, it felt as if something was going to happen while the king and warriors were away. He had looked forward to a peaceful summer with his friends. The foreman wouldn't dare drive them hard, even if he wanted to.

He had to be ready day and night for what might come. He didn't know where it would come from; it might be directed at the farmstead, but it would most probably be leveled at him.

Long rows of oar blades flashed in time with a rhythmic shout, and the ships glided past the pilings, followed by the waving and shouting of the people on shore. A little ways out, the sails filled and the oars were pulled in. The dragon heads gaped toward the town, and in the stern of each ship stood a steersman. White water soon foamed at the bows; the ships would be in town in no time.

Holme's wife and daughter approached him on the narrow path along the ditch. He saw them clearly as if for the first time and consciously rejoiced in their existence. But he had a sense of foreboding at the same time. He wouldn't be able to live in peace with them much longer. In the calm, which spread across town and land after the fleet's departure, lurked an unknown danger.

It was too early to begin the day's work so they rested a while longer. The farmstead seemed deserted. Tora walked to the door several times to see how far the ships had gone. Holme noticed how much she had filled out in a very short time. Since the festival of sacrifice, she had also been more restless and uneasy than before. He knew, of course, what that meant; he had seen many people grow up and mature. But she was going to decide for herself—no one was going to rape her, as he once had her mother. Holme smiled at the memory and looked at Ausi's supple arm resting close to him. Rape, though, it could hardly have been called that time. He remembered well enough that arm encircling his neck once she gave up resisting.

Tora finally lay down on her bed, and soon all three of them were sleeping as the sound of the whistling birch trees made its way through the smoke vent.

When the sun reached its zenith, Holme headed home from the smithy to eat. Ausi had just called out that dinner was ready. He looked across the lake toward town, but there was nothing to see. The queen and her companions still hadn't returned. She might stay in town until the next day.

As he walked in through the low door, he noticed something move at the edge of the forest. He stopped and could soon make out a figure sticking up out of the thicket. It motioned to him. After a moment's reflection, he picked up his ax and walked over. Mother and daughter came out and watched him in surprise. The figure disappeared as Holme started moving toward it.

The free thrall was joyfully waiting for him behind the thicket. Holme was happy too and surprised to see him. The thrall told eagerly what had happened and was happening at the old settlement, and Holme soon breathed more easily. He had expected the worst when he first saw his old battle companion.

He took his friend to his house, where both Ausi and Tora were happy to receive a visitor. At the table, he continued his story and Ausi smiled warmly and broadly at his drowning Svein's mother, her old nemesis, like a rat that morning. He suggested they should kill the stiff-necked son too; then they would be rid of anyone who could lay claim to the farmsteads. He didn't notice Ausi's reluctance, or Holme shaking his head, or Tora's eyes flashing angrily at the suggestion.

Holme felt happy again at the thought that there was a thrall who had become free and independent. He had shown himself worthy of freedom; he had worked hard and was prepared to fight for what he had gained. Maybe no one had to fight this time; maybe the matter could be settled peaceably. Holme thought of the boy who was now the sole owner of the farmstead and who had offered him his hand at the spring sacrifice. They would go and talk to him. Maybe he would hand the farmstead over on conditions the thrall could accept. It was worth trying anyway, now that the fierce, wicked mother was gone.

But Holme couldn't leave right away to help his old friend. He was responsible for the king's farmstead, and both the queen and the foreman had to give him permission to be away for a few days.

The thrall insisted that the easiest thing to do would be to kill the son. But his vision was limited; he was afraid of losing the farmstead, but he couldn't acquire the farmstead and land by killing its owner. That had been done many times before, of course, and would happen again, but it would always bring bloodshed and death. Neighbors had to live in peace and help each other.

And when the free thrall returned to his loved ones satisfied, he had Holme's promise to follow along soon. In return the thrall had to promise not to do anything against the other farmstead and its young owner. They'd seek a peaceful solution first; if that didn't work, they could think about other alternatives.

Holme walked with him to the hidden boat, feeling happy all the while about his friend's freedom. The others he had tried to help hadn't really understood what he had meant; they'd expected things to be done for them and complained when they hadn't had something. They were dead and buried now. They hadn't understood that they had to be strong to be free. The one walking beside him was strong and knew that you had to work and fight for freedom. Such men had to come first and then gradually teach the others. But even so, you shouldn't kill someone for his farmstead or goods; you should just defend what's yours. His friend would soon come to understand this.

The morning's premonition of hard times had passed for a moment, but when he saw the thrall row out alone in the little boat, the feeling returned. There were only two of them, and strong, ancient powers stood against them. One day, it would be their turn to be killed and their hope would vanish as it had come. Freemen didn't believe in a life without thralls and didn't want to hear it talked about.

Holme was puzzled about why he thought of these things when

such a peaceful time lay ahead of him. The king and the warriors were gone; those who had stayed behind worked peacefully and offered sacrifices for the new harvest and the raid's success. But there was a cloud somewhere. He felt it more clearly now than ever before.

Filled with something close to certainty, he walked straight to the smithy to check his weapons. Locked inside an iron-bound chest was a stash of finished weapons, which the king kept in reserve. He opened the lid and looked at them. They might come into use sooner than anyone expected. He shook his head at the thought and locked the chest. It might be that he was just unused to going very long without fighting and being pursued.

Svein heard one of the thralls give out a yell and then point toward the edge of the forest. There stood two figures, looking down at the new building. When they noticed they had been discovered, they walked calmly down the slope.

Svein looked at them and suddenly found it hard to breathe. They were both huge men, but there was something about one of them that was hard to pin down. He had felt terror because of it before, but now he joyously threw his tool aside and hurried to meet them. All work stopped, as everyone turned toward the newcomers. They saw Svein extend his hand to the biggest man and then, after some hesitation, to the other. Svein wondered what had brought Holme to the farmstead. Could his mother have started up the old chase again? But Holme looked peaceful, and his eyes were calm. It had to be something else. But he didn't ask. Instead, he showed them around the building, talking as they went. Holme greeted the thralls as he passed them. Some who had known him for a long time beamed with happiness; the others watched him, their eyes filled with curiosity. The lumber worker started walking with them, too, talking and pointing. The house would be ready soon; they had begun putting on the finishing touches. It was a bigger house than the one the pirates had burned on the same spot.

All the while, Holme was figuring out the best way to explain why he was there. He had agreed with the free thrall that they shouldn't mention the mother's death. Neither did Svein ever need to know how it had happened, even if someone found her. No one had seen the free thrall knock her out of the boat.

When they had seen everything, Svein looked expectantly at him. Well, he naturally had to know something important brought them there. The free thrall would probably have preferred to let his ax do the talking so he could feel confident about his farmstead, but that's not the way it was going to be.

After a while, the three men sat down on the slope, and a thrall was ordered to bring beer from a container in the grove. The workers watched curiously, undoubtedly wishing they were with them to hear what was going on. Holme was pleased to see that thralls were treated well here, too; the young man talked quietly to them and worked as they did. His hands were dirty and black from the resin.

It was strange sitting there opposite the old master's son. Still stranger that this son wasn't like his parents. He had been a sulky, ill-tempered boy before, but now he had a different look and a different attitude toward his thralls. There must be something behind that change, but what?

Although the man listening to him was very young, Holme began his story far back in time so that he would understand what was going to follow. He explained how the thought of freedom had started and was the cause of everything that had happened since. Like the king before him, Svein saw that Holme had done only what he had to do. He would have done the same. Holme had defended an ideal, as well as his family and friends, against violence and injustice from the freemen. It pleased Svein that this was so, and he was proud that the feared Holme, Tora's father, sat beside him, talking to him man to man. And he remembered that he knew Holme wouldn't be dangerous if you approached him without guile.

Svein longed to hear Tora's name, but he asked nothing. Then he heard that the man at Holme's side had lived at his relatives' farmstead and had worked it for a year, that the man wanted to stay there, and that he was the first free thrall. All the others had been killed and were buried behind the town.

Both men's eyes were directed at Svein as Holme talked, Holme's with friendly expectation but with something else behind it, something that called forth a shudder from Svein's childhood. Something that told him that he was too little to stand in the way of this thought of freedom. The free thrall's look told him more openly that denying the request could be dangerous. But once Svein had understood what they wanted, he had no desire to say no. He was glad Holme was asking something of him, and he had no problem about the relatives' farmstead. His father's was enough for him. His thoughts settled for a moment on his mother's wrath, but only for a moment. If she made a fuss, there was still the hut in the grove. She could just sit there, locked up, again.

Holme said further that they had no intention of taking anything from him. Once the free thrall had gotten on his feet and the farmstead was supporting itself, he would pay for it in a way they could agree on. That way the naysayers could see that neither thralls nor fighting were necessary. That was the most important thing.

And Svein shook both their hands in agreement. He didn't understand yet how all this would come about, but he felt friendship in that mighty hand. The free thrall was surely the one who had shot an arrow at him, but that didn't matter. It was easy to understand why. The thrall's face was friendly and happy now, too. He could stay at the other farmstead with his wife and child. And both farmsteads would stand under Holme's protection.

Holme was surprised but also relieved that the young man was so agreeable. He sensed something behind this, but not cowardice. He remembered the morning of the spring sacrifice when he had found Svein outside his house and Tora's face in the window. Maybe his thoughts were constantly on the girl. It was very unusual for a freeman to become attached to a thrall girl, even a girl like Tora. He remembered, too, that Tora's eyes seemed quizzical when she heard where he was going and that he planned to see Svein. It just might be that the children of old, deadly enemies harbored warm thoughts for each other.

Holme smiled, sensing again that a great deal in his life had taken its own course. And now the young man asked about how the mother and daughter were. Holme heard himself answer that Svein should visit the king's farmstead when the time was right and see about their well-being himself. He saw happiness in the young man's eyes and thought that too could be a stage in the fight for freedom. A young freeman was voluntarily and respectfully approaching the thrall class.

It was clear to Holme yet again how much had changed since he had been a thrall at the settlement under Svein's father. The short-legged chieftain lay in a burial mound down near the cove. The son didn't look like him; he was of his mother's sort, taller and lighter. But his disposition was better than his mother's; it was open and friendly. It hadn't always been so – he had been an obstinate and hard boy. But something had happened to change him. Maybe his departed relatives were looking after him, making him wiser and better than his parents.

Svein still bore the mark of the stone that hit him in the neck when he was a child. But it was less noticeable now that he'd grown up. Holme realized with surprise that he wouldn't exact revenge on a child now even if its parents had done him great harm. But he had been young then and Tora had been abandoned in the woods to die. It was more merciful to die by being hit in the head with a rock than by being eaten alive by ants, flying insects, wolves, or wild boars. Freemen always had an edge even when it came to cruelty and hardness. So what did they expect from thralls?

They soon said goodbye to the young man, who walked a short ways into the forest with them. The free thrall, full of happiness, wanted Holme to spend the night at his place, but Holme already had other plans. He'd been thinking about his old friends in town, the smiths, and thought it couldn't be too dangerous now to pass by that way to visit them. They'd be surprised, and it made him glad to think of seeing them again.

Late that night, Holme reached the ferry station. The same oarsman was still there, but he had grown old and gray. Twice he had ferried Holme across, fearing for his life both times, and his eyes bulged anxiously beneath his bushy eyebrows now, too. As he rowed, he tried to ingratiate himself with Holme as he talked about everything that had happened in town since the last time. But Holme didn't like his cowardice and responded only with an occasional growl, as he had before.

Not many people were moving about in the harbor and only a couple of larger ships were there – merchant vessels from foreign lands, and some fishing boats and small skiffs. Some of the older townspeople stopped and stared at the massive figure who stepped ashore and paid the oarsman. Although he was better dressed than before, they couldn't mistake who he was. And they hurried off into the quiet town to spread the big news. He walked toward the craftsmen's part of town where his smithy once had been.

Holme felt strange walking in freedom through this town where so much had happened to him. He had been the master smith. He had been sentenced to death. He had led an uprising against the Christians and had torn down their first church. It had all happened without his wanting or planning it.

He saw that most people recognized him. The freemen kept going, puffing with excitement, but some of the thralls came up to him with pleasant words and friendly eyes. A few followed him as before, forgetting what they were supposed to be doing. Perhaps they still hoped for the freedom that he had once tried to give them. He noticed one thrall's back striped with whip marks, and he felt the old hatred moving deep inside his chest. At the same time, the feeling that he had deserted them returned. Things were going well for him, but his friends were still being whipped and tormented as before. Maybe he needed to get away from the peace and quiet of the king's farmstead after all. But not before the king came back. Holme had promised to look after his queen, children, and possessions. And the king was a good master.

There were many new smiths in the smithies, but the old ones gathered around him, buzzing with happiness. Black, powerful hands reached out to him, and voices assured him that if they had known his life was in danger in the fortress last year, they surely would have come to his aid. They talked with admiration about the time he had killed Geire and his men with his bare hands and had gotten away. The battle god, the most powerful of all the gods, had to be on his side, no matter what he thought.

Their words pleased Holme, but he realized that when the time came, the smiths might not be on his side. They were independent men not much bothered by the plight of the oppressed thralls, and while they would defend themselves, they wouldn't raise their sledgehammers for many others. They had forgotten that their independence had begun during his tenure as master smith and that they had once been mistreated thralls themselves.

But it was still fun to see them again and see what they were doing. A couple of the oldest ones walked back with him and wanted to lend him a boat for the trip to the king's farmstead. The streets were livelier now than they had been moments before. Faces kept peeking out everywhere, around corners and through doorways. Mothers called their children in and slammed their doors. Having heard the news, Svein's mother positioned herself where she thought Holme would pass by. She had summoned the Christian priests, but they were nowhere to be seen.

Holme saw the woman on the street corner and felt a mixture of fear and wonder. It was the woman his friend had drowned a few days earlier. He had never before seen anyone return from the dead and felt very uncomfortable. You couldn't do anything against the dead, so, to the smiths' surprise, Holme dragged his friends across the street. When they had passed the woman, though, she sent a shrill stream of insults after them, and Holme looked back at her. She must be alive after all; the dead kept their silence and didn't insult you, and didn't show themselves in town either. The free thrall had to have been wrong, or she must have swum ashore without his noticing it. The thought made Holme breathe easier. But it would be more dangerous for the free thrall at the farmstead now since the mother wouldn't be as agreeable as the son. It would have been best for everyone if she had drowned.

While he was still talking with the smiths on shore, a number of people from town came down. Most of them stood a little ways away watching them, but some came up and said hello. They were mostly thralls, but some of them were merchants who had been there when Holme was the master smith and considered a freeman.

Many people talked at once as they tugged at his clothes. Thralls complained about their masters and asked for help. A freeman asked him to head up a fight against the Christians, who had become more and more entrenched and robbed the women while their men were out at sea. From a distance, the Christian priests themselves approached, followed by a group of women and some older men. Svein's mother was right next to the priests. They stopped a little ways away, and the woman pointed directly at Holme.

The priests looked curiously at the man who was the biggest obstacle to their progress in town. They had expected a wild animal from the primeval forest and so looked with wonder at the smiths – three powerful men. It must be the youngest of them who was Holme. The heathens crowded expectantly around him.

Holme was a little taller and more powerfully built than most men; otherwise there was nothing noteworthy about him. The priests said to each other that people had exaggerated his significance. That dark man would no longer stand in the way of the light. And they moved closer to show how little they feared him.

Holme was ready to step into the boat when he heard the woman's shrill, hard voice. He had heard the charges before, but now the woman was hoping for speedy justice. Indicating the priests, she said that they were more powerful than either the chieftain or the king. They and their god had promised to stand by her.

The priests hadn't intended for things to turn out this way.

They had just wanted to see the feared thrall and form an opinion about him. They had done that, and now they wanted to quiet the woman down. It was clear that everyone standing with the smith was ready to protect him. It wasn't the right time yet, but a better one would present itself.

They heard Holme tell those around him that he had to go back to the king's farmstead, but if they needed him, if there was great danger for them, he would be there. But he didn't expect any such danger. And he shot a glance at the priests and their following of women before stepping into the boat.

Both priests felt more at ease after seeing that their enemy was an ordinary human being. He seemed almost shy as he stepped into the boat, and he didn't respond to the woman's insults. The priests walked down to the water as he rowed out, one of them observing contemptuously something about such an insignificant enemy soon being brushed aside.

Holme could only catch the tone of the priest's words, and it irritated him. Would these priests always make his life difficult? He stopped rowing and looked the priest straight in the eye. The priest thought for a moment that the ground had disappeared from under his feet, and the words he intended to add to what he had said never came out. He didn't positively know what he had seen in the smith's eyes, but it had to do with death. Holme was clearly more dangerous than he looked.

The heathens called after him to come back soon, and Holme promised more willingly to do so, now that he was irritated. Then he rowed with powerful strokes to get away from the place. He didn't want anything to happen that the king wouldn't like. When the king returned, it would be time for Holme to make his position known. If he didn't want to hear what Holme had to say about the thralls, then Holme would probably have to resort to his old ways.

His peace of mind soon began to return, though. A number of good things had still happened in his life, after all. Still better and still calmer would it have been had these gray Christian priests not, time after time, come to his land with their new god. They spread unrest among the people, and there was conflict and bloodshed wherever they went. And their god was insatiable. He wasn't satisfied with animal sacrifices but had to be appeased with silver and gold.

Holme could see the big gray buildings of the king's farmstead and his own smithy in the clump of birch trees. The lake was shimmering and everything was peaceful. Soon, Ausi and Tora would come running to meet him.

He didn't see anything he needed to be afraid of. Even so, the voice of uneasiness continued whispering inside him – this calm was foreboding. It wasn't the first time he had felt a dark premonition mixed with the sunlight itself. But this time he didn't know where the wind would be coming from.

Holme looked to the mainland forests and momentarily felt his old longing to walk into the depths of the woods and stay there until he died. But he had two women to answer for, and many thralls with backs torn apart by the whip were expecting his help. He couldn't think about himself. The looks the Christians gave him also told him that they hadn't forgotten what he had once done to them.

Then he saw mother and daughter running to shore, just as he had expected. Maybe a few days would pass before something happened. The queen waited every day for a call to arms from the king, and sacrificial smoke was rising into the sky now. She was in the shrine making offerings to the gods so they'd give the king good fortune on his raid. That might be necessary after all; there'd been many bad signs lately, both on the earth among the newborn animals and in the heavens. The old conflicts between Christ and the wooden gods couldn't do an undertaking like this any good.

Holme would be glad when he saw the king's sail fill the horizon. He was a good king, and as long as he was alive there was hope for the thralls. After he was gone, no one knew what was going to happen.

During the next few days, two more Christian ships came to town. The priests had frequent business to do with them, even after they had taken ashore what they needed for their work. And the two ships, which Holme had seen in the harbor, stayed there, although they'd been ready to sail for a long time.

On their way in, the newly arrived ships had heard a rumor that the Swedes had failed on their raid. First a storm had forced them ashore on the foreign coast, and then the town defenders had attacked them. There were only splinters left of the ships, and most of the men had been killed or taken prisoner.

The priests interpreted these events with thanks as Christ's doing. He had finally shown that He was the Lord. The heathens left at home would give in now and seek baptism in terror and desperation. But the Christians did not spread the news of the disaster. The heathens wouldn't believe it unless they heard it from one of their own.

The priests knew, however, that a powerful group among the heathens wouldn't give up, no matter what happened. That was why there was whispering on the Christian ships and furtive glances cast toward shore. Through trickery or violence, they would strike the heathens to the ground in the name of Christ, and their abominable temple would be burned. And without followers, the Christians' biggest enemy, the smith at the king's farmstead, would be almost harmless. The homeless thralls Holme could gather were both weak with hunger and unarmed.

So the plans were formulated while they waited. The new female converts, whose husbands would never return, were bound closer to Christ by the thought of a reunion in heaven. The priests were no longer saying that Christ would bring them back safely. Once news of the catastrophe reached town, many of these wives would give all they owned to save their husbands' souls from the flames of hell.

The disquiet grew, both at the king's farmstead and in town. It was midsummer, the nights were already a little longer and darker, but there was no message from the king. A smaller ship had been sent out to search, but it hadn't returned either. The heathen priests scrutinized the entrails of the sacrificial beasts but found no clear sign about what had happened or would happen.

The hostility between the Christians and heathens intensified. The Christians walked around looking scornful or self-important, as if they knew something or were certain of victory. And their numbers grew. The merchants from the foreign ships refused to deal with or exchange goods with the heathens. People insulted each other's gods, and it occasionally came to violence.

Then one day during the harvesting of leaves, a few men appeared at the ferry on the mainland. They were thin, and their beards were long and wild. You could hardly tell if they were thralls or warriors, although a couple of them carried swords, and gold trim sometimes flashed from the tattered and torn clothes. Except for the oldest of them all – a stately, gray-bearded man – they seemed dismal and forlorn. Those who couldn't get a place in the ferryboat took boats themselves without asking the owner's permission.

You could see the three small boats from town, and many people walked down to the harbor. Everyone had been waiting with mounting excitement for news, and many had checked every boat that came across. That's how it had been for a long time. The queen was in town often, spending hours standing on the rocks by the fortress, looking across the water. But it had been barren and blue with eternally rolling waves.

Shortly after the bearded men had stepped ashore on the island, the harbor was buzzing with people. Some of the women recognized them and let out cries of joy. But most of them wept silently and disconsolately when they learned that the others were gone, probably forever. The chieftain went straight to the queen when he heard that she was in town. The king was among those who had been captured and taken away.

The chieftain's eyes were calm, and it looked like he had known all along how the raid would turn out. When the storm came up, he had encouraged the king and the men to turn to Christ, but they had refused and started offering sacrifices to their wooden gods, whose statues they had on board. Only he from his ship and then these men had been saved, after casting their wooden gods into the sea and calling on Christ. He had dragged them up on an islet after their ship had been dashed to bits on the enemy coast. After the enemies had gone inland toward their town with prisoners and goods, a merchant ship had picked up the shipwrecked warriors and put them ashore a long ways from the town. They had endured many hardships traveling home.

Everyone in town knew all this shortly after the men stepped ashore. The Christian bell summoned the people and a column of sobbing women hurried toward the church to demand their husbands back as the priests had promised. But a number of the new female converts looked toward the church with hatred. They had all the while counted on Christ to return their husbands alive. They didn't know what heaven was, but they did know anxiety and felt compassion for their husbands, who had gone to the land of the dead unarmed and without provisions for the journey.

The heathens weren't idle either. The heathen priests understood at once that the wooden gods had allowed this misfortune to beset their people because so many still worshiped Christ. Their patience gone, the gods would surely destroy them all if people didn't return to their fathers' faith and drive the Christians out. The muffled beating of drums was heard from the heathen temple and people streamed there, too. On the way Christians and heathens exchanged derisive words and an occasional punch or kick. Women on both sides were wailing out their accusations.

Bell and drum competed constantly, and both temples were soon filled with believers. The gray-haired chieftain came last, after taking his tale of calamity to the queen. The Christian priests received him joyously and interpreted his being spared as a sign of victory. After a thanksgiving service, they would confer together about the best way to deliver the death blow to the heathens.

In the heathen temple apprehension and suppressed rage reigned. Everyone agreed that a message had to be sent inland immediately to the main temple. The gods had to be appeased with a greater sacrifice than usual, perhaps with human offerings, if everyone wasn't to be destroyed. And the Christians in town one way or another would have to pay for what they had started by provoking the wooden gods.

Someone brought up Holme, and the name glided like a whisper through the heathen temple. Many faces brightened and the apprehension changed to confidence. Here was a man who stood in the middle between the camps of the gods, someone whom Christ had no control over and whom the wooden gods seemed to favor despite his not offering sacrifices to them. The king was gone now and it was because of the Christians. That alone would kindle Holme's wrath against them. And he wouldn't have to fight alone this time. They would send out a secret call to arms to everyone who still believed in the ancient wooden gods.

And that same day, the heathens started marshaling their forces. Boats set out in all directions with the message. The homeless in town and the surrounding areas were summoned and catered to, treated well so that when it came down to the battle, they would be on the right side. But the town's defenders at the fortress said that they intended only to do their duty – defend the town against external attack, wherever it might come from. They'd have no part in a war between the Christians and heathens.

The Christians were in full swing now, too. Everywhere among the heathens, there were those who had a foot in each camp so they could get help from either direction when danger threatened. Many of them now hurried to the Christian church with the news. When Holme was mentioned as well, the gray-bearded chieftain knew this could be serious. Would there never be an end to the smith and his actions?

And when the chieftain walked through town, he noticed that something was afoot. The heathens were standing around in groups and some of them said aloud that the old gray-bearded Christian chieftain should have been the one lost in the east instead of the good king. And thralls, who had once scurried out of his path, now dared face him and stare him in the eye. Someone must have said something to give them such courage.

The chieftain kept going toward the fortress. The shipwrecked warriors were there, with new clothes and weapons, still devouring food like wolves after a long famine. Their wives sat outside the guardhouse, happy the men had been spared. The chieftain encouraged them to remember who had saved their husbands – it had been Christ and no one else.

He told the warriors what the atmosphere in town was like. If the heathens attacked the Christians it was the warriors' duty to defend them and the town. The king had promised the Christians his protection, and their priests came from a powerful land. If they were killed, an army could come and destroy the town in revenge.

The shipwrecked warriors agreed with their chieftain when he said that Christ was the one who had saved them from destruction. If they hadn't been on the same ship as their Christian chieftain they would be lying on the bottom of the ocean now or in the hands of the enemy, which would be even worse. They intended to fight on the chieftain's side if the heathens wanted battle.

The town guards showed reluctance for a long time, but when the chieftain left them, he knew they'd follow his orders. They were strong men, used to battle, and the heathens were mainly merchants, craftsmen, and thralls. With Christ's help, the heathens would be quickly defeated.

The chieftain felt satisfied and gave thanks in his heart to Christ. He had forgotten Holme for a moment, but on the way back, the thought returned so fiercely that the chieftain stopped in his tracks. He had heard that the smith had been in town a few days before. Holme shouldn't have gotten out alive.

Maybe it would be safest to seek the wolf in his den. There was no one at the king's farmstead who could stand by him. A few warriors could quickly dispatch him.

But the chieftain drove the thought away and walked on. Maybe Holme would stay away. He ought to be glad to be alive after all he'd done and ought not to get mixed up in another fight. The king wasn't around to protect him now, either.

The most important thing was to protect the lives of the foreign priests. They wouldn't be allowed to show themselves in town without guards as long as there was unrest. An arrow could come silently flying from a window, or a paid thrall could be waiting around the corner of a building with an ax. They were his responsibility now until an assembly could be summoned and a king chosen. Even if Christ was big, He couldn't be everywhere to defend His followers.

Women came up to the chieftain wherever he went, wanting some word about their missing husbands or sons. He told the Christian women gently that their men were in safekeeping with Christ, but he hissed angrily in his beard at the heathen women when he told them that their husbands were burning in hell. Most of them looked at him uncomprehendingly and repeated their question.

It was calmer in town now than when the chieftain had walked to the fortress before. The heathens might still think twice and wait for the assembly. He would summon it soon so that they would have something to think about besides the Christians. Meanwhile, he would confer with the Christian priests. It might be best to attack before the heathens could gather their forces.

In the church, the chieftain found the priests busy packing all the treasures to load onto the ships. They would be safer there than in town, if it should come to a fight. The rich woman was dead, and they had figured out just how many more prayers for her soul her silver would justify. Her daughter and heir looked on silently, and the priests again said something about the treasures she had laid up for herself in heaven.

No one working on the new building knew anything about smithwork, so Svein decided to go into town to order what was needed. He was also thinking about his mother, who had been gone for several days. It would be best to take her away from town with all her hatred and rage. She couldn't do much harm at the settlement.

The lumber worker went with him since his work was done, but the others stayed to clean up. A number of them had promised to stay at the settlement when they saw that they would be treated almost like freemen. Svein wanted to pursue Holme's idea and couldn't understand how he had thought completely otherwise before. He hoped, too, to get over to the king's farmstead while he was in town. A face with a friendly, teasing smile and bordered by black hair was constantly in his mind.

The ferryman immediately told them what had happened to the king and his army. He also said that people were coming to town from every direction and pointed at a few small boats being rowed toward town. The wooden gods had commanded that the Christians be driven from town and land for all time. Otherwise, a foreign army would come and destroy everything, kill all the men, and take the women and children captive. The unrest in town was great.

Svein didn't reply but thought that Holme must be in town, and he wanted to be at his side, no matter what happened. He felt his chest expand with lust for battle. He would show them that he was no coward. And after the battle he would follow Holme to the king's farmstead and see Tora again. With a great feeling of happiness, he turned his stiff neck and looked across the water toward the king's farmstead. Svein heard the lumber worker say something about his son – he had been along on the raid in the east. He'd never see him again. He was dead or captured.

Svein knew that the gathering place was at the heathen temple and went directly there. The most prominent merchants were there and the hall was full of armed men. But the Christian church was buzzing with people outside too. Threats and shouts of derision went flying across the courtyard between the temples. Svein searched for Holme, but he was nowhere to be seen. He soon heard Holme's name, though, and understood that they had just decided to send a message to him. Full of zeal, he offered to go himself, and many men turned toward him with scrutinizing eyes.

Svein was soon chosen to go. Some said that his mother was Holme's bitterest enemy and that the son might dump Holme in the lake, but the others smiled at these words. And so, forgetting the smithwork, Svein walked happily to the harbor, accompanied by two powerful oarsmen. Someone shrieked his name from the Christian church, but he neither answered nor turned around.

Holme saw the queen step ashore and walk to the farmstead, followed by the women of the court. She covered her face once as if she were crying. Her figure had gotten a little heavier. She would surely have a child this winter. A vague memory came back to him – he somehow recognized the movement when she put her arm over her face and he felt a momentary urge to caress her stomach. But the feeling soon disappeared before the others that pressed in upon him.

A while later, someone came running to the smithy with the rumor. Holme listened silently to the story and could then understand the darkness that had been blended in with the sunlight the past few days. The good king would not return, and then peace would come to an end at his farmstead, too. The wolves would remember and emerge from their dens. The man carrying the rumor walked on and Holme mechanically opened the chest to look at the masses of weapons for a moment. A row of new axes hung on the wall, and he walked along the row looking at each of them without understanding why. Howls and laughter from the king's children would occasionally press in through the open door, creating a strange atmosphere. Since none of the king's sons was grown and could take over for his father, a new king had to be chosen quickly. And probably a new smith at the king's farmstead.

Several things lay there half-finished, but Holme's desire to work was gone with his master. Why should he forge anything when he didn't know what tomorrow would bring? If they chose a Christian king, he had to flee – the priests' looks had told him as much when he had passed through town.

Holme stood by the door looking out over the bay. Uneasiness gnawed at his heart, joining with a feeling resembling grief over the good king. He had never had a chance to talk with him about the thralls' misery, and now it was too late. Who would understand now?

A boat appeared far in the distance, the oars glistening as they were lifted from the water. Holme had a feeling that this had to do with him. It was someone who needed his help or maybe someone who wanted to warn him. Anything was possible now.

The boat approached rapidly and Holme walked down to meet it. He sat on a beached log as the warm summer wind played in his grizzled hair. Ausi and Tora were standing outside their house with their hands shielding their eyes from the sun. It was on its way down and the water glistened. The king's children had been called in and the farmstead was completely silent. A cow's mooing came drifting across the water from some distant place.

The boat changed course when its occupants caught sight of the massive figure on shore. Holme wasn't surprised; he knew they were on their way to see him. When they laid to, he got up and walked toward them. Svein greeted him happily, and a hint of surprise finally flashed across Holme's face. He had expected someone else.

As Svein relayed his message, he kept looking up toward the two women outside Holme's house. Holme noticed that, and a little smile flitted across his face, despite the gravity of the news. Followed by the three men, he walked up toward the house to tell his wife and daughter the news. Holme had already decided to go back to town with the messengers. His master was dead, and the queen was in no danger. He could leave the farmstead for a while.

As he talked with Ausi inside, the two young people stood outside. They didn't say much to each other. Svein mentioned something about the building work, and the girl watched him furtively. He had grown since she had seen him last, but beside Holme he had still looked like a boy as they walked up toward the house. Tora had turned away so her mother wouldn't see how glad she was about the visit.

Inside the house, Holme was just as taciturn. All Ausi found out was that he was going to town because the Christians were posing more and more of a threat. But surely, nothing bad would happen. He'd be back soon. Ausi and Tora ought to stay home.

The farmstead's foreman, who didn't like the king's making Holme his equal, didn't mind seeing him step into the boat. Neither did he care when they carried a chest and a bundle of axes from the smithy and loaded them into the boat. All the better if the smith never came back. The new king didn't need to know anything about him.

He saw Holme's wife and daughter saying good-bye to the men at the shore. He wasn't close enough to see the brown and blue eyes meeting hastily, parting, then meeting again. Or to see Ausi and Holme exchange a knowing smile. Ausi couldn't understand how just the sight of Svein had once made her feel uncomfortable. It must have been the painful memory of slavery at his parents' settlement. But the young man was good and reliable. Maybe sometime when she and Holme were gone. . . .

And she imagined Tora as the mistress of the settlement. They wouldn't leave any thrall descendants behind, she and Holme. And she wouldn't want to live even for Tora's sake if Holme died. She had known that for a long time. She had to be there to tell Christ how good Holme was under that dour exterior. The Christians had surely lied about him, and Christ couldn't be everywhere Himself.

As the men pushed away from shore, Ausi's heart felt heavier than it had in a long time. Things had been much worse than this many times before without her feeling this dark foreboding. It could be because they had been living in peace and safety at the farmstead. And she and Holme weren't so young anymore, either.

The thralls rowed; Holme and the young Svein waved farewell. Svein felt as if he were already part of the family. He regarded Holme with great admiration and respect, and Ausi and Tora had to like him just for that. He didn't even have the freeman's arrogant way of looking at ordinary thralls.

As mother and daughter returned home, some thralls yelled from the fields to find out what had happened. Ausi explained as well as she could, and they looked pensively toward town. One of them said that Holme should have taken them along. Everything was up in the air here since they had heard that the king would never return to his farmstead. No one knew how the new king would treat his underlings.

The foreman looked at the root crops, and the thralls bent down again toward the earth. But as soon as they could straighten up, they looked toward town and wondered what was going on there.

Nothing seemed unusual when Holme, Svein, and the oarsmen stepped ashore. Some of the town's heathen merchants and craftsmen met them and seemed to breathe easier at the sight of Holme. They believed that the Christians bore evil in their hearts against them, but they didn't know what they were planning on doing. The last few days, many people had gone to the side of the Christians, who had never been so strong before. And the town defenders would join them. The heathens wanted to hear what Holme intended to do – shouldn't they attack the Christians when they were off guard?

But Holme didn't want to start any fighting. Defending yourself was another matter. And the Christians had the king's promise to live and hold their services as they wished. It would be better to wait and see what the Christians' intentions were. He'd stay in town until all this was over.

And that's what they did. They walked up toward the temple, a crowd of people behind them. As usual, a number of thralls came up to Holme, complaining bitterly. And he knew that if a fight broke out and the Christians were defeated, the slavery question would be taken up once more. The Christians always said that thralls meant as much as freemen to their god, but they still treated them cruelly and beat them as often as the heathens did. From them, you could expect nothing.

Many eyes, both curious and threatening, from inside the Christian church followed them to the heathen temple. Four men carried the heavy chest of weapons, and two followed with the glistening axes. The Christian chieftain thought bitterly of stepping out and ordering them to put down their weapons, but the priests stopped him, and he saw immediately that that would have been premature. The heathens would have responded with an attack, and the time wasn't right yet.

The chieftain and priests had noticed preparations for a sacrifice going on in the heathen temple. The heathens might be drunk around midnight, and that would be the time to attack and tear down their repulsive temple. They didn't dare burn it; it was too close to the church and the town buildings. If, on the other hand, they could goad the drunken heathens into an attack, that would be much better. The responsibility would then fall on them.

The priests administered the holy communion as they waited, and the whole time the kneeling Christians kept hearing the sacrificial animals at the heathen temple braying and mooing through the priests' mumbled words. They soon sensed a faint smell of smoke, too. The war between the gods had begun.

Boats kept coming from every direction on the mainland. One, two, or three men stepped out of each of them and walked toward the heathen temple. Some were armed; others came almost without clothes on their bodies. A Christian or two came as well and walked with dignity into the church. The door was immediately shut after them, but the hall of the heathen temple was swarming with people, completely visible to all. Raucous laughter came frequently from there, cutting strangely through the Christian solemnity.

Holme wasn't happy about all these preparations. He understood that the heathen merchants were friendly because they needed him. They knew that the Christians hated and feared him, and that the thralls followed him wherever he went and looked up to him. But he was uncomfortable about how everything was being built up for a battle and knew that people would expect him to fight without provocation.

The whole time, people around him were talking about the Christians' shameless ravaging after they found out that the king and his warriors wouldn't return from the raid. They didn't even balk at leading small children into the church and baptizing them. The children had gone home to their mothers with water running from their hair and told what had happened.

Holme also heard about the rich woman who had given everything she owned to the Christians, who had said there weren't any poor people in town, not even in the whole land. And he thought about all the misery he had seen, about all those who were starving and freezing. There were decrepit thralls all over the town and environs, old men and women, who had been driven away when they could no longer work. They slept under the open sky and covered themselves with whatever they could find. They searched for food in the town's garbage heaps. But the Christian woman sent her treasures to a foreign land.

Holme felt more fatigue and bitterness than anger at the thought of all this, however. Someone brought him some beer, and he drank it to get out of his bad mood. He watched the heathen priests smearing the wooden gods with sacrificial blood, but that was none of his business. Svein stayed at his side the whole time, and many old acquaintances among the thralls kept near him, talking proudly about past battles with the Christians. He couldn't desert them if it came to a fight.

Many warriors had come from the fortress and were wandering around aimlessly. They kept close to the Christian church but didn't go in. Some cast a stealthy glance at the bloody wooden god who stood at the front of the heathen temple. He had helped them in battle several times before, but now he would stand against them. His standing so far forward in the hall indicated that the heathens were expecting battle.

Both inside and outside the temple, thralls were milling about. It wasn't often they could move around so freely, and they enjoyed pretending they were freemen. They were needed now, and no one drove them away from the places where they otherwise couldn't set foot. The warriors watched them with disdain from the other side, commenting among themselves that they didn't need to be called away from the fortress for adversaries such as those. But inside the temple, there were well-armed merchants and craftsmen. There, too, was the man everyone was thinking about but no one was mentioning.

Holme listened to the head priest trying to incite the men to war. He listed the Christians' misdeeds and described the unrest they had caused in the town and the land. He criticized the two kings who had let them into the land.[11] Both were gone now – and now the time was at hand to drive the Christians out. Everything indicated that this was the gods' will.

These words stuck in Holme's mind, and his thoughts moved back in time. The priest was right about what he said – the Christians had brought unrest and strife. And it had to be because of them that the good king and his men were dead and gone. Either the Christian god had sent the storm that destroyed them, or they had provoked the wooden gods into sending it.

Outside in the courtyard, the crowd of people was growing larger and larger. Someone said that the crews on the foreign vessels had come and joined the Christians. The church door was open now, and there was a light of some kind inside in the darkness. But in the heathen temple, the sacrificial fire was burning cheerfully, crackling and reeking, and from outside you could see everything that was going on in there.

There was some hesitation among the Christians. They were prepared for battle, but the heathens had to seem like the aggressors to everybody. The chieftain and priests conferred together on the best way to bring that about. They couldn't be certain of victory either. If they had only the heathen merchants and priests against them, they would soon overpower them. But the temple swarmed with half-wild thralls, who were excited with beer and who did whatever their dangerous leader told them to do. Without him, it would be easy to scare them off.

Should they try yet again to get their hands on Holme? The

11. I.e., Björn and Olaf.

merchants could be threatened with the wrath of the yet unchosen king. And the smith was, after all, already guilty and sentenced. The law had to be obeyed, justice served.

A short time later, the chieftain was standing outside the church, surrounded and protected by the town's defenders. The news moved quickly into the heathen temple, and everyone streamed from the hall into the courtyard. Many of them were hoping for a fight; others preferred to avoid one. In the middle of the hall stood Holme.

The chieftain began to speak. He said that Christianity, which had been victorious in so many lands, would now be victorious among them, too. Its power could not be resisted. The new king would be a Christian, and then the era of the wooden gods would soon be through. This should have happened a long time ago, as it had in neighboring lands. No powerless wooden gods – devils, more like it – were there any longer.

The chieftain further suggested that they should try to avoid the battle that was threatening them. Many lives would be lost for no reason. The Christians didn't want any man's death, but rather each and every man's conversion and salvation. Only one man stood in the way of all that, one sent by Satan to stand against the power of the light. And the chieftain pointed at Holme, whose head and shoulders rose above the surrounding crowd.

A murmur passed through the rows of heathens, but it grew quiet again as the chieftain continued. He outlined Holme's life, and again it sounded as if Holme were the biggest criminal in the land. The heathen merchants looked pensive again. The chieftain noticed that and promised that no one would be forced to be baptized if they turned the smith over to him of their own free will. The heathen temple could stay put until it was clear that the wooden gods' power was ended.

The chieftain finished with yet another suggestion. Everyone knew Holme was a strong and dangerous thrall. To save lives, the heathens should capture him themselves and turn him over to the Christians. Afterward, all would be peaceful and everyone could go back to their own business.

The chieftain had spoken with authority, and he was the most prominent man in town. The heathen merchants and a great many of the craftsmen looked around, not knowing what to do. They looked at Holme out of the corners of their eyes, but his face was unchanged except, perhaps, that his jaw was jutting out a little more than before the chieftain's speech.

One of the thralls who had understood the speech stepped closer to Holme and looked at him with probing eyes. The others followed suit and he was soon standing in the midst of them. The merchants' sporadic words came to him over the heads of the thralls – there was something to what the chieftain had said – he hadn't lied; maybe it would be best to come to terms with the Christians again. Fighting wouldn't do anyone any good.

Holme could smell the thralls around him and looked at their rags. Beyond them, the merchants' eyes were looking around evasively, doubtfully, partly hostile. He began to understand that the fight wouldn't be between heathens and Christians but, like before, between freemen and thralls.

His chest immediately felt lighter when that dawned on him. This wasn't a new battle; it was the same old one. He was in his place again. He saw the chief merchants walking into the courtyard and the chieftain and Christian priests meeting them. They would reach an agreement, and he'd be the prize. The head heathen priest pushed his way through the group of thralls up to him, his face full of anxiety, and he urged them to fight. The wooden gods would help them gain victory; all the signs were favorable.

The priests and temple attendants would fight, too. And the message had gone out the day before to the inland temple. Help would soon be on its way.

Holme listened to the head priest as he looked around. Closest to him stood Svein, armed, and you could see by his look that he stood firm. Some of the thralls had huge sticks, some had axes, but most were unarmed. He understood better now why he had brought along the king's weapon chest. Followed by a curious group of thralls, he walked to the chest and opened it. The thralls snatched up the new swords with delight. They had never laid hands on such things before. Many of them preferred axes, the thralls' ancient tool and weapon.

The heathen merchants returned from the courtyard, and you could tell from their falsely grinning faces that they had agreed to the chieftain's conditions. Except for one thing. They didn't want, or didn't dare, to take Holme themselves. Behind them came ten men whom the chieftain had sent from the town guard, men with arrogant faces.

Holme followed all this as if it concerned someone else. He still wasn't sure what he wanted to do. He was waiting for something to happen that would clarify the situation. That's how it had been before. Something always happened when the time came.

He noticed that many of the thralls watched the approaching warriors with terror. They were used to beatings and whippings, to bending their backs and suffering. This wasn't easy for them. He himself felt that his life's toughest battle still remained to be fought and was close at hand. Maybe he would be alone – the thralls at the front looked back plaintively. He glanced out into the courtyard and saw the priests' and chieftain's faces. They were happy and already certain of victory.

That was what he needed. He felt the rage rise now, and with it, his strength. The victory might be the Christians', the thralls might die, but not alone. Some of the freemen would be carried up to where the burial mounds were at the same time as others dug holes and buried the thralls like dogs. He'd make sure of that himself.

But he still wanted to wait. The merchants, who had first called on him for help and then turned him over to the Christians, now stood at the edge of the courtyard to see what would happen. They believed the Christians' promises. One would die for all, now. He might have given himself up of his own free will if it meant saving his thrall companions. But he had never been able to believe the promises of freemen to thralls. They didn't have to be kept.

A powerfully built man forced his way through the crowd, panting. He reeked of beer, his eyes were glistening with happiness, and Holme, too, smiled with joy. It was the free thrall. A message had reached him and he had come at the last moment. Someone had described the situation to him, and so he now stood proudly by Holme's side. To those standing closest to him he boasted that this wasn't the first time he and Holme had fought together.

All the while, the temple attendants kept bringing beer for the thralls and the craftsmen who were on the heathens' side. At a call from the chieftain, the warriors had stopped outside the temple hall – the chieftain and the Christians wanted the heathens to attack so that the responsibility would fall on them. The heathen priests noticed how hesitant the thralls were and knew the beer would increase their lust for battle. Their number grew constantly and the newcomers were given swords or axes. The heathen priests started believing in victory and loudly promised their gods greater sacrifices than ever before.

From his position, Holme could see that the Christian church was filled with women. He was glad that there were no more of his enemies than the men he saw in the courtyard. The heathens' own women were nowhere to be seen. Not many of the thralls had women, and by old custom women ought not to be around when danger was threatening.

A man from town appeared now, insulting the gods of the land with a loud voice. He said they were ridiculous and weak, and challenged them triumphantly to strike him to the ground if they could. He looked defiantly at the blood-smeared wooden figures, but nothing happened, although a tense hush wafted over the courtyard. It was broken by the heathen priests' call to their gods to let something happen. From the other side rose a voice calling on Christ to demonstrate His power.

None of the gods had any desire to listen to their children but instead left them to settle their own affairs. The old chieftain grew tired of nothing happening. He had seen the thralls retreat, and he again ordered the warriors to move in and take Holme. Cut him down if it didn't work any other way. Or were they afraid of a thrall?

When Holme heard the order, he knew the time had come. He forced his way to the front, followed by Svein and the free thrall, who laughed from the beer and his lust for battle. It was also he who started the fight because of his arrogance. He took a piece of flaming wood from the sacred pyre and hurled it at the warriors. It hit some of them, and they let out an angry roar. Sparks and smoke danced around them. The thrall laughed loudly and scornfully, and some voices joined in from the hall behind them.

But then the warriors balked, looking uneasily at the pack of stick-, sword-, and ax-swinging thralls in rags. They were pretty dangerous, and unworthy opponents besides. The smith was standing before them, but it was no easy matter to go up and take him, even if he were alone. The first man, and probably several more, would never see another sunrise.

Behind the ranks, the chieftain quietly gave an order to a row of archers. The heathens had attacked by throwing the burning wood, so the Christians could start defending themselves. The archers stepped up on a small rise, the strings twanged, and the arrows flew into the temple hall. Most of them flew too high, and one thumped against the chest of the battle god and fell to the ground. Screams showed that others had hit their marks. A half-naked thrall with an arrow in his shoulder pushed his way up to Holme. Groaning, the thrall looked up to him for help as a child would to his father. Behind the group of Christians, the archers drew their bows again.

When Holme attacked with the free thrall and Svein beside him, he thought vaguely that he wasn't like he had been before. Then, he would have charged on all by himself if no one would follow him, but that kind of rage hadn't come this time. It was the pitiable look from the wounded thrall that finally forced him into action and freed him from his long hesitation. Behind him, the call of the heathen priests urged them on to battle, and they had armed themselves, too. In the opposing camp, the Christian priests were unarmed. When the fighting began, they stretched their hands into the air and called aloud to their god.

The second shower of arrows hit those at the rear of the group. The number of archers had increased, and in the midst of the growing tumult, Holme understood the danger. The warriors had closed ranks when the thralls approached, but had kept their ground. If the group of thralls, unused to battle, stormed out into the courtyard the warriors could attack from the rear or take them from the side. The heathen merchants stood off to one side by themselves. They talked eagerly, waving their weapons, probably still unable to agree about which side to join.

The warriors had silently agreed that the half-drunk band of thralls was almost harmless without its leader. If they could strike him down first, the way would be clear. But no one wanted to go up against him. Even if a number of them rushed him at once, at least a couple of them would lose their lives. That was too high a price to pay.

After a moment's consultation, the warriors had figured out the best thing to do. Someone brought out a cudgel of juniper wood almost as long as a man was tall. They would keep it hidden, and when the thralls attacked, their leader would be struck down before anyone got within reach of the thralls' axes.

The free thrall stormed past Holme in his eagerness for battle, and they were all soon out in the courtyard. The warriors stood there like a wall, but when the thralls were on top of them, they quickly opened ranks and the polelike cudgel rose and fell. Holme saw it coming and tried to dodge it, but it hit him in the side of the head and glanced off his shoulder. He felt a hard jolt and intense pain and simultaneously saw the look on his old battle companion's face – a look both anxious and surprised.

The pain made him go berserk, and he charged straight into the warriors with his ax raised. Behind him came the thralls, yelling and roaring, and the warriors at the forefront retreated as their ranks fell into disarray. Two or three fell before Holme's and the free thrall's blows, and the others moved back, fending off the fury of the thralls. The archers couldn't shoot for fear of hitting their own men.

During all this, Holme sustained another blow against his wounded shoulder and saw the blood flow. One of the warriors had hacked him with his sword this time. He raised his sword again, but it never came down. Holme smashed his chest with his ax, then watched the man fall, his mouth wide open. An instant later, Holme saw Svein trying desperately to defend himself against one of the Christian warriors, and he rushed to his aid. The man tumbled heavily to the ground and a panting Svein looked thankfully at his rescuer.

The head priest in the heathen temple grew anxious after a while when he saw the thralls' attack slacking off and gradually stopping. They hadn't been trained to use weapons, so they were swinging them too hard and tiring themselves out. Those with axes were doing best. He saw Holme charge ahead like a wild man, bloody and torn, but the thralls didn't know enough to follow him and kept scattering more and more instead. The shouts of the Christian priests and the chieftain had the ring of victory to them, and someone soon started clanging the church bell. The thralls, confused and surprised, watched it out of the corners of their eyes as they were being driven back toward the heathen temple.

The heathen priest quickly gathered the temple attendants around him and told them his plan. If it didn't work, they'd soon all be dead. The Christians wouldn't show any of the mercy they boasted about so much if they were victorious.

The group of priests and temple attendants was soon sneaking out a back way and hurrying along the wall and past the courtyard to come out behind the Christians' quarters. Some men came running from the edge of the town to join them. From inside the Christian church came the gentle hum of female voices singing. Following the heathen priest's directions, about half the assailants sneaked to each side of the church, then with a wild howl, jumped the Christians. The archers were the closest but didn't have time to use their bows; they had to throw them down and draw their swords instead.

The retreating thralls took heart when they saw what was happening. Holme, Svein, the free thrall, and some others were still fighting in the courtyard, and now they got some relief. The heathen merchants, seeing the battle going against the Christians, took part now, too. One after another of the Christians turned and fled past the heathen priest toward the church. The chieftain yelled angrily at them to hold their ground, but to no avail.

After a while, the courtyard was in the hands of the thralls, and the Christians stood crammed together in and around their church. The warriors' ranks had thinned, but those still there were ready to fight on. But even the thralls had had enough, so the battle stopped. There were no taunting yells now; the wounded crawled toward their people for care and protection.

The heathen priests were disappointed that the fighting had stopped without the Christians being killed and their church destroyed. They tried to incite their people to attack again but the lust for battle was gone. The heathen merchants were satisfied with the Christians' being driven back despite all the talk about their god. The wooden gods stood victorious in their hall, showing that they too were not to be taken lightly.

An old priest came up to Holme and put an herb dressing on his wounded shoulder. The sword wound wasn't too deep, but he had lost a lot of blood. The Christians looked on from across the courtyard. They hadn't managed this time either to take this dangerous man's life, despite their trickery.

The heathens had won the battle, but the victory was small. Holme had wanted the fight to be for the good of the thralls, but instead it was they who had fought for the wooden gods. That's how it was, no matter how you looked at it. They had fought well, but it didn't mean anything would change for the better for them. Even so, the time should be right now, when not so many warriors were there to overpower the thralls.

He gave a hard look at the heathen merchants who had waited until they saw which way the battle would turn before taking part. They were the ones who profited from the victory. The thralls never won – whenever they worked or fought, it was for others. Holme was gripped by a rage greater than what he felt during the fight, and when a couple of the heathen merchants approached him smiling, he turned his back on them and walked in among the thralls.

Holme thought that the heathen priests had shown greater courage than the merchants. And after the battle, they were friendly to the thralls, saw to their wounds, and gave them meat, bread, and beer – probably because they were glad that the Christians had been driven back. Had the Christians been victorious, the heathen priests and he would have been the first to be killed.

Then Holme saw one of the heathen priests, a scornful smile on his face, walk out into the courtyard and dip a branch into the blood of a Christian who had fallen in battle. The Christians let out angry shouts when he walked up to the wooden god and smeared it with the blood. He went back to dip the branch again, but an arrow came flying at him and he jumped quickly out of its way, raised his fist at the Christians, and ran back into the hall. There were shouts and rattling weapons on both sides, and it looked for a moment as though the battle would begin all over again.

Yet again, Holme was surrounded by thralls with their weapons and their rags. They looked happy about the victory. Maybe they thought it could mean better things for them. Several had come to him, childishly but proudly telling him what they had done during the fight. He had a feeling that he himself had fought worse than ever before, but it wasn't clear to him why. But when the thralls' fight came one day, it would be different.

Svein and the free thrall stood beside him, and he praised them both. Their eyes began gleaming with happiness, and they talked about what they'd do if the battle began again. And Holme thought about those times when he had had to fight alone. Now, though, many pairs of eyes looked at him with confidence, many weapons would be raised at his word.

The Christian priests had watched the battle from the church steps, the women singing behind them. When the battle turned against them, they said it was because so many of them must be just nominal Christians. They secretly sacrificed to their wooden gods and made promises to them. But Christ, who saw into the heart, had allowed this setback to come to pass as a warning and punishment.

But the chieftain, who was a warrior, said that the setback was because of Holme. He had armed the thralls and led them. Without him, they could have been driven off like a flock of sheep. The heathen merchants would probably have given up without the thralls' help, and the priests then could have been overcome and killed. It was Holme alone who stood between the Christians and ultimate victory. With him gone, the setback would soon be reversed.

The chieftain withdrew with the priests into the church to discuss a new way to relieve the thralls' leader and protector of his life. Someday they were going to find him alone and unarmed. Or maybe there was a weapon he wouldn't know how to defend himself against. And the three men started whispering, their heads thrust forwards.

A while later, two women came running across the courtyard toward the heathen temple. They were panting and said they were tired of the Christians, who hadn't brought their husbands back to them as they had promised. They wanted to return to the gods who had shown themselves to be the strongest in battle. They were eager to serve those in the temple in whatever way they could.

One of them was young and beautiful, but the other was older and hid her face in her kerchief. Svein watched her attentively as she followed the priests and the young woman into the temple. That the younger woman could serve the gods as women usually did in the temple, that he understood, but what could the older woman do? Well, that wasn't his concern and besides, there was a need for such women to wait on the men.

The heathen priests were elated about their success and weren't sparing with the beer. They invited Holme and those around him into the temple, and he walked in after posting a strong guard. The Christians had done the same. They probably wouldn't attack but would wait instead to see what was going to happen. Many of their women were standing outside the church now, looking toward the temple. A number of them might want to walk across the courtyard in order to serve the gods. The fertility god was standing at the front of the temple now, smiling, his organ jutting into the air.

The two women were already at work waiting on the men. The older one poured beer while the younger one served it. She smiled when they grabbed her, having completely forgotten her promises to the pure and cold Christ.

The older one kept her back to the temple entrance for the most part but stole an occasional glance under her kerchief. She started breathing more heavily when Holme came in, then busied herself a moment with a pitcher of beer. When the younger woman came back, she whispered something to her and gestured meaningfully.

Holme was the first to get some beer, then sat on a bench fastened to the wall. The woman looked at him timidly. She came right back with beer for Svein and the free thrall who sat beside him. The thrall was still happy and suggested that they should drink to the thralls' victory and freedom.

Over the top of his tankard, the thrall saw the older woman sneaking a look back at him from under her kerchief. A wild and evil delight was flashing from her eyes as she stared at Holme, and then the thrall recognized her. He dropped his tankard to the floor, and Holme lowered his in surprise, wondering if his friend had had enough.

The thrall, speechless with terror, got up and pointed at the woman. He had drowned her, but there she stood. Holme immediately understood the thrall's terror; he pulled him down on the bench and told him that the woman must have swum ashore or been rescued. That wasn't a dead woman he was looking at.

Many of the people standing there had followed the events and heard what Holme had said. They began staring at the older woman and noticed that she fumbled around more and more, and that her hands were shaking. The young woman was still walking around among the men, but her smile had become rigid and her hands shook too as she handed out the tankards of beer.

Holme had finally become suspicious as well. A couple of women couldn't do much harm, of course, but the Christians certainly had sent them to find out something about the heathens' plans. When the head priest came over to him, he suggested that the women should be gotten out of the temple.

The older woman thought that this might mean her life. So she took off toward the door, her clothes flapping, screaming triumphantly that Holme would soon be a dead man. What many men couldn't do, she had done alone.

Everyone was surprised at her words, but in the beginning no one understood what they meant. The woman fluttered through the hall and out into the courtyard. The younger woman tried to follow her but was seized by the thralls. She was panting. Her terror-filled eyes were directed at Holme, and she said something about their making her do it.

The head priest questioned her while Holme stood by silently. She told him that the Christian priests and the chieftain had decided to poison Holme's beer. The older woman owned both him and his family; they had done her great harm, and she would gladly volunteer to walk to the heathen temple with the poison if she could have a younger woman to go with her.

Everyone stared in horror at Holme, and the free thrall in a rage lifted his hand against the woman. But Holme stopped him, showing his tankard. He had taken only one swallow before the thrall had dropped his tankard. It surely couldn't be enough to kill him. The thrall, Svein, and the others were jubilant. The priests smiled, too, and one of them hurried after an antidote.

The older woman had escaped, but the younger one was still there, quivering with fear in the thralls' hard grip. The head priest said that Holme should determine her fate, but he shook his head and walked away. He dumped the beer in a corner of the down-trodden dirt floor and a trickle ran out into the open. He felt a little sick and drank quickly from the tankard with the antidote in it that the priest handed him.

Meanwhile, the head priest wondered what to do with the young woman. He could see that many of the thralls were eyeing her lustfully and decided to hand her over to them, but on the condition that they take her on the fertility god's altar. The thralls slipped happily away with her, and she had an expression of relief on her face when she heard she'd be permitted to live.

For a long time Holme sat, his face severely contorted and his hands clutching his stomach. The priest skilled in medicine kept urging Holme to drink more beer. Svein and the thralls crowded in around him, anxiously watching his face. Svein looked away toward Freyr's Hall a few times, imagining what the thralls were doing to the woman, and that made his body tingle with excitement. He didn't want her, but he did want to watch.

The free thrall stuck close to Holme. He reproached himself bitterly for not having made sure that the witch had really drowned. Next time, he would see to it that she wouldn't cause any more trouble. Holme smiled weakly and looked at Svein standing beside him, but Svein didn't seem to care much about what happened or could happen to his mother.

The chieftain and the Christian priests listened gleefully to what Svein's mother had to say. She had seen the dangerous man drinking the poisoned beer, so he would surely be dead soon. Without him the pack of thralls would be defeated easily. The warriors could see to that all by themselves.

They looked across the courtyard for a while, hoping the younger woman could manage to escape, too, but time passed and there was no sign of her. She was probably dead. The priests prayed for her soul not knowing that it was her body that was in the most peril just then. And they never found out that she stayed in the heathen temple of her own free will after she had taken her punishment and the men had grown tired.

Svein's mother was finally seeing her moment of justice and revenge approaching. Her son was still with the heathens, but that didn't bother her – he would probably come home to the settlement once the battle was over and the Christians had won. Out there, they could cleave to whatever gods they wanted to. But first, with the help of the Christians, she would get the smith's wife and daughter. They were going to find out that their protector was no longer there.

She could see and feel the mood brightening among the Christians. The heathens had posted a guard and withdrawn into the temple – something had to be happening inside. Almost all of the heathen merchants had gone home and surely wouldn't get involved in another fight. They had shown how fickle they were the last time. True, more and more thralls kept streaming to the temple, but what could they do without their leader? There probably weren't any weapons for them either. Their axes and clubs didn't amount to much against arrows, spears, and swords.

Far to the front above the altar, Christ hung on a cross. His head was bowed submissively, and he didn't seem to care about the battle. The warriors, who occasionally looked curiously into the church, were contemptuous of him, but some of the women looked at him with tears in their eyes. All the warriors saw was a defeated wooden god, but maybe the women felt something else for him.

The chieftain had known that Holme had fought not for the wooden god, but for the thralls. The strange notion that the thralls should be freemen and -women would disappear with him and would never be allowed to rise again. If it survived its originator, it would be struck down.

Bodies lay in the courtyard, and the chieftain gave an order for them to be carried into the church. But they should be careful not to take in a heathen along with them. The Christians laid their dead unburned in a graveyard some distance away from that of the heathens. They were buried with their faces pointing east, the direction from which Christ would be coming to awaken them. Heathens always cremated their dead, but gave them food and drink nonetheless for the journey through the land of death.[12]

The chieftain had kept careful track of everyone leaving the heathen temple. There were only a few craftsmen and merchants left now, apart from the thralls. Their number grew constantly, but their leader had to be dead. A big, smiling thrall had fought fiercely by his side, but he probably couldn't take Holme's place and lead the others in battle.

They would wait for nightfall and see what would be best to do; the heathens would probably have a feast and make offerings to their gods for the victory, despite losing their leader. After they had drunk a lot of beer, they would fall asleep and forget all about keeping watch.

A fleet of dragon ships, their unfamiliar sails furled, came gliding through the archipelago. It approached from the east, since a king there had heard that the wealthy town's ships and armies had left. There couldn't be many warriors left to defend the town. And as far as the king knew, no one had plundered it for many years. He had turned his ships around and sailed day and night with the dragon heads gaping toward the west.

He had known for a long time that the fortress was nearly impregnable. But if they could approach the defense works from another direction, they could surprise the handful of defenders.

The king was a Christian and had priests on every ship. They had assured him that Christ was with them in attacking the town where inhabitants still stubbornly clung to their ancient wooden gods. A number of Christians had lost their lives there, and their blood had been smeared on the terrible wooden idols. That abom-

12. Some debate exists over the question of Viking burial practices. Although some scholars argue that the dead frequently were buried intact, others argue that in the area in which Holme lives, cremation was the rule. See Schön, *Fridegård och forntiden*, p. 115.

ination had to be stopped and the king should stop it while relieving the town's merchants of their silver and gold at the same time. Christ had brought them a favorable wind, and the water foamed around the bows.

The king knew the channel well, and he found to his surprise that the fire wasn't burning on the rocks near the fortress. Someone might have been there before him. Or the inhabitants might not fear any danger because summer was coming to an end and everyone had to be home harvesting crops. The fire might just have gone out for a short time, too, and could flame up again at any minute.

He had his men lower the sails and row carefully in on the far side of the island. They couldn't land there, but his warriors could wade quietly through knee-deep water. The town was well-protected on the harbor side.

The raiders carried various objects with them from their ship – things that could help them get past the fortifications. They were soon there without being noticed. Whispering to each other, they climbed over the wall between two watchtowers. No one sounded the alarm – no shout, no horn blast, no church bell ringing. The town was quiet, except for the murmuring from the temple, and a veil of smoke rose toward the reddish-blue night sky in the west.

One after another, the Danish Vikings appeared for a moment on top of the barricades, then disappeared inside. There were no guards in the towers, none on the gangways. Something must have happened for the town to be left so unguarded. The Vikings smiled in satisfaction, happy that Christ was with them. After a while, they stood by the hundreds inside the barricades, checking their weapons one last time.

A couple of merchants who lived nearby were on their way home, content with the day's events. The Christians had been defeated without the expense of much blood or silver. Mostly thralls had fought and mostly thralls had fallen. That was good. No one had thought before that thralls could be used for fighting, not just for working. Now it would be nice to live in peace and quiet for a while. A king would soon be chosen, and they hoped he'd stay home and build up trade with the large kingdoms to the south.

The two merchants heard strange sounds from the craftsmen's side of town for a moment without thinking much about it. But a figure suddenly popped up on the barricades and disappeared again. No normal figure – silhouetted by the moon, which had just come up behind him, he had horns on his helmet like a bull.[13] The merchants whispered a few terrified words to each other and ran back toward the temple. This was going to be much more serious than the day's battle between Christians and heathens.

In the middle of the courtyard between the Christian church and the heathen temple, the merchants stood panting, yelling out the bad news. Men rushed out from both sides to hear what was happening. Some of the thralls reeled merrily about, not really grasping the problem, but the Christian chieftain walked quickly to his warriors and started organizing them for battle. They looked immediately more alive and pleased than before. They'd finally get to do their duty, something worthy of them – defend the town against invading Vikings. They had taken part in the fight with the thralls only out of necessity.

The chieftain was angry at himself for not having thought of

13. The popular notion that Vikings wore horned helmets cannot be supported by archeological evidence, all of which suggests that the Viking helmet was conical. Horned helmets may have been worn for ceremonial purposes during the Bronze Age and pre-Viking period, but the evidence for that is slight as well. See Graham-Campbell, *Viking World*, p. 24, and Bertil Almgren, ed., *The Viking* (London: C. A. Watts, 1966), p. 221.

this. The town's helplessness had to be known out on the high seas, so he should have foreseen what was happening now. He could only hope that it was a small fleet of pirates they could handle, and that the thralls and other heathens didn't throw in with the enemies. That had to be prevented.

So the chieftain ran into the middle of the courtyard. In a thundering voice he roared out the news and said that they all had to fight for the town. Otherwise, every man would undoubtedly be killed and every woman raped. They knew well enough what would happen. It made no difference whether the raiders were Christian or heathen.

The heathen priests saw that the chieftain was right. Everyone's life was at stake here, Christian or not. The invaders surely wouldn't find the valuables that could be brought together in the town a sufficient ransom. So they had to fight side by side with the Christians.

Holme still wasn't himself, but he followed everything being shouted in the courtyard and hall. And the head priest soon panted up to him to explain how things had suddenly changed. For now, they had to fight; afterward, they could settle accounts with the Christians in town.

As Holme followed him out he heard him whisper a promise of great sacrifices to the battle god if he helped them out of this fix. Dark-red Christian blood was still dripping down from the god. Outside in the courtyard, the chieftain was arranging his warriors the way he wanted them. He said they would wait for the enemy up here so they could take advantage of the slope. And if the enemy won, they had the fortified walkway to the fortress to escape through. They were closer to the gods here, too, both to Christ and to the terrible idols in the temple.

A gasp of surprise rippled through the Christian ranks when

Holme stepped forth from behind the gods. The chieftain's words stuck in his throat, and his mouth hung open. But he quickly recovered himself and repeated that everyone had to fight those who had already gotten into town. He added that the thralls would not go unrewarded if they performed well. They had recently shown they could handle weapons.

Holme thought briefly about what he had been singled out for by the Christians just moments before. That was probably the reward thralls always would get. But he'd remember the chieftain's words and remind him of them after the fight. He would suggest the only proper payment – they should set the thralls free, or at least treat them well. He would also refresh their memories about how the fallen king had treated his thralls.

But first they had to defeat the enemy. If the invaders won, they'd plunder the town, kill the men, and maybe set all ablaze before moving on. Then they'd probably head for the king's farmstead. And that meant Ausi and Tora.

With that thought, Holme knew the thralls had to fight. They were already crowding around, looking at him expectantly. The chieftain observed all this from the courtyard with intense interest, maybe even anxiety. Without Holme and the thralls, or with them at their back, the Christians had no hope of defending themselves or the town.

The invaders seemed to know where the town's defenders were. A strange bull head appeared for a moment around a street corner, and an indistinct murmuring arose from down in the town. They could hear light openings being carefully opened and slammed shut by lone, frightened women. Holme thought it best to charge down the slope and attack before the enemy had a chance to regroup, but the chieftain would decide that. He was hurrying the women and children onto the pathway leading into the fortress.

But the enemy had no desire to wait. All at once, they swarmed howling and roaring up the slope. The Christian archers let their arrows fly, but there were far too few arrows to stop them. The chieftain's warriors stood like a wall against the enemy, and the street was too narrow for the attackers to force the defenders into the open courtyard. Swords flashed and clanged. The warriors seemed to launch immediately into a battle frenzy that they hadn't mustered against the thralls a few hours earlier.

To his joy, the chieftain thought they would manage to beat the attackers back. The thralls stood behind them in reserve and hadn't been needed and couldn't even take part in the battle. But things soon changed. A strong troop of invaders, who couldn't find room in the street, had gone around and now came rushing in from the other side.

Then the chieftain saw something in the midst of battle that struck him with surprise. The thralls' leader had seen the turn of events at least as quickly as he had. With a yell, he summoned the thralls and charged the new attackers. The chieftain could almost see the enemy's astonishment when they met a ragged, wild band with axes, swords, and clubs. Many of them were laughing and unsteady on their feet. The chieftain couldn't follow the thralls' battle anymore, but he saw a constant stream of them rush from the temple and cast themselves into the fray.

When Holme saw the invaders coming to attack from the rear, he knew how great the danger was. And before he even had time to think, he had the thralls with him charging against the attackers.

But he could soon see that their adversaries were powerful. As soon as the bulls recovered from their surprise, they began coldly and contemptuously hacking down the impassioned thralls. They parried the thralls' blows skillfully and responded instantly, with dire consequences.

Holme saw his drunken companions fall bleeding on both sides of him. He was gripped by despair and rage over their helplessness against the well-trained, experienced enemy. Followed by Svein and the free thrall, Holme plowed ahead, hacking away with his huge ax. The invaders began leaping out of the way of this raging giant, having soon perceived that parrying did no good here. His reach exceeded theirs, and the power in his blows made their weapons fly from their hands. Some of the thralls regained their courage and together with Svein and the free thrall shielded his flanks.

Holme was no longer thinking about what he was up against; he only wanted revenge on those who were killing the thralls. More thralls rushed to his aid from the temple than those who fell, and the enemy was slowly pushed back. A few of them could see that it was the raging leader who gave the others courage. If he fell, the others would soon take flight. But no one could take him from the front, and his companions protected him on all sides.

Seeing the troop of thralls continuing to swell, the horned invaders began to lose courage. Several of their own lay on the ground, dead or wounded by blows from the thralls, and they began to see that victory was not certain. It was better to flee from thralls than to fall from their blows. One after another sneaked away from the hind ranks to run for the boats. Holme saw this and burst forward with renewed rage. But the whole time he could feel his wounded shoulder holding him back.

More and more enemies fled in a lumbering gait down the slope to escape over the barricades to the safety of their ships. The thralls' howling became triumphant and their attack more wild. Their side of the courtyard was soon empty, and the hunt raged down the slope. The last opponents to have held their ground

170

were fleeing now, and the thralls chased them to the edge of town. Some stopped to relieve the fallen invaders of their weapons, clothes, and jewelry. The battle god watched it all with a grin from his hall, his fire still burning. Some priests who had taken part in the chase came back to the temple, panting and smiling.

Meanwhile, the main body of the invaders had pushed the town warriors back a good distance, but they couldn't help seeing what was happening to their comrades on the other side. They were afraid that they, too, would be attacked from the rear, and they withdrew as they fought. One after another broke ranks and ran for the edge of town and the ships. The Christian chieftain knew that the town had been saved and hoped that Holme, with his thralls, would know enough to stop the retreat.

But even if that was Holme's thought, he couldn't make himself heard any longer. The thralls had gone wild with success, and many of them clambered rashly over the barricades to chase the invaders on the other side. But the enemy was waiting with weapons ready, and it was an easy matter for them to skewer the thralls who came jumping or clambering down after them.

Holme could hear from the outside what was happening, but couldn't do anything about it. Nearby stood a watchtower with a gate, and he grabbed the men closest to him and rushed over there. The guard wasn't there, but they hacked at the gate with their axes and soon broke through it. Followed by some thralls, Holme rushed out. The enemy who saw the thralls' huge leader coming didn't dare wait for him but ran toward the shore instead. Below the barricades lay some wounded thralls, writhing in agony, and Holme stopped. He thought fleetingly that with more experience in battle, they would never have chased the enemy over the barricade. Many thralls were going to have to pay with their blood for the day's victory.

There was tumult again, as the main body of the enemy rolled out through the shattered gate. The town warriors were tight on their heels and Holme thought he should probably join in the chase. But that could cost more thrall blood. They had done their part in defending the town. Now the warriors would have to do what remained to be done.

Holme picked up a wounded thrall in his arms and headed toward the temple and the priests, who knew something about medicine. The others followed his example, and soon there were no thralls left at the barricades. Only a few dead remained, lying still in their blood and rags.

All along the road to the temple lay the enemy dead or wounded. The thralls plundered them, hitting them in the head with clubs if they resisted. Holme watched them but said nothing. They had as much right to the enemies' possessions as the warriors did, and they needed them more.

From the shore came shouts and the sounds of battle. The head priest smiled at Holme, pleased that he had not stayed with the chase all the way to the ships. Still more Christians would be felled by the retreating enemy, and that was good. He had noticed that the attackers were Christians, too, and they could just as well kill each other while their god sat indifferently in their church, his head hanging.

As the invaders fled, the old Christian chieftain himself led the chase. After a tough skirmish on the shore, they managed to capture two of the ships while the others were being manned and rowed out. There were many dead and wounded from both sides lying on the shore and in the water.

At first it annoyed the chieftain that Holme and his thralls weren't there for the end of the battle, but that didn't bother him after a while. Victory belonged to the Christians now. They knew inwardly that they would have been lost without the thralls, but probably no one but the thralls' leader comprehended that.

The Christian priests, who had watched the last battle from a distance, came up to the chieftain. It was clear to them that Christ had a hand in the enemies' attack. What would happen now was unclear, but it would soon be revealed. Everyone, though, had seen how He even used thralls for His purposes. And His worst enemy, the leader of the thralls, had fought for His sake.

But all three thought with mortification about the same thing. Everything would have been so easy if the thralls' leader had fallen in the battle. But he lived, and he'd surely demand payment for what the thralls had done. And the thralls were strong enough to take up the fight from the temple yet again. They might get help as well from the main inland temple. The Christians knew that a message had been sent there.

The chieftain thought, too, that there was no longer any order in town. An outlaw thrall had led his fellows into battle. Such a thing had never happened before and there must be an end to it. The king was dead, so the chieftain was responsible for everything. A king would be chosen, but he had to be a Christian. The band of thralls had to be struck down before there was a vote.

As they walked up toward town, past fallen and plundered enemies, he talked with the priests. He knew that their way was right when they said they had to proceed with trickery. The heathens had proven too strong to strike down after they had accepted help from the thralls. Now the thralls had to be gotten rid of, and that would be an easy matter with their leader out of the way.

That said, the three Christians looked at each other. The poison hadn't affected Holme; maybe it was Christ's will that he should die violently because of the violent man he was.

And they decided that that was how it was going to be. For now, they would go along with his demands, in order to lull him into a sense of security. The right time would come later.

The wounded were still being carried across the courtyard to both temples. They saw a priest put a poultice on Holme's shoulder and exchanged a look of satisfaction. He had been wounded and that was a good sign. They were on the right track.

A hundred thralls were standing around Holme; many of them were wounded. When the chieftain and the priests entered the courtyard, the thralls turned toward them, and a sea of clear, childish, demanding looks washed over the chieftain. In the middle were Holme's watchful dark eyes; hundreds of others surrounded him. The chieftain felt uneasy. What did they want from him? They had defended the town, but that was everyone's duty. Given enough warriors, he would have commanded them to drive that ragged pack from town.

The priests sensed his anger and encouraged him to have patience. There had been enough fighting; they shouldn't provoke the children of the wooden gods again. He should pretend to accept their conditions for Christ's sake. Christ would then give them into the Christians' hands.

They walked into the church to say a short prayer of thanksgiving. Across the courtyard the battle god grinned contentedly at being smeared anew with enemy blood. The thralls got more meat and beer while Holme thought silently about what he should do. The Christian chieftain would surely not go along with his idea. There was probably nothing left to do but fight yet again. All too many thralls had fallen — those who were living had to have recompense of some kind for them.

But a short while later, the chieftain was standing in the courtyard speaking. His voice was friendly and he was praising the thralls' fighting. It would not go unrewarded. For now, though, they should all keep the peace and look after the wounded on both sides. They could reach an agreement later. Those who wanted to go home could do so quietly. He wanted Holme's and the head priest's word that they wouldn't violate the peace. He was giving his own word.

Holme was surprised at the mild tone and reasonable words. Would they finally win something without further fighting? The head priest gave him a look of secret, mutual understanding. It meant that they knew how to make promises – but then what?

As evening approached, Holme decided to go to the king's farmstead for Ausi and Tora. They were probably living in dread, and it could be pleasant for them to visit town. He smiled when Svein beamed as Holme went on his way.

The head priest followed him to the edge of the courtyard and urged him to return soon. The Christians couldn't be trusted. Holme should be back early the next morning.

But many of the Christians had left the church and gone home, too. They surely weren't thinking of attacking again. They had many dead and wounded, maybe more than the heathens had.

On the other side of the courtyard, they tensely watched Holme leave and some hasty orders were given. A few pairs of eyes reflected hesitation or terror, but finally obedience. Then several pairs of feet went running into the distance.

Dim light, flickering, fading. A shout in the distance. A memory trying to force its way to the surface and take shape.

Eventually he could hear leaves rustling in the wind and could slowly turn his head. The grass was thick in front of his face. He was on the ground, unable to get up.

After a while, he tried again and managed to roll on one side. Something stuck up out of the long blades of grass in front of him. An arm and a hand. Someone was next to him.

Ill-defined images came and went just as the light had. There was danger nearby. He strained again and got onto his hands and knees. Then he could see the whole man lying there motionless, ashen-faced. He saw a pool of blood on the ground around him, still flowing from him. But he felt nothing.

He looked around from his huddled position. Was it night? In the distance the sky was red, but it hurt to look at it. He saw another man lying in the grass behind him, and a little to one side, another. Not one of them moved. Maybe they were sleeping like he had been.

He started crawling away from them through the grass. He didn't know how far he had crawled before there was another man in his path. But this man's eyes were open, and he moved. Holme had a feeling that this was the danger he had sensed. And he started crawling straight for the man.

When the wounded man saw the bloody smith crawling toward him, his eyes gaped with terror. With great effort he rolled one turn away, but his pursuer crawled after him. He managed another full turn and then half. His face was to the ground when the iron fingers clenched his neck. A moment later, he was as peaceful as the other three.

After a while, Holme crawled on. He tried getting to his feet several times, but kept falling down. Soon he saw a stone in front of him, a stone that stood among the burial mounds. It was taller than a man and he had seen it before. He clutched it, steadied himself, and managed to get up. For a long time he stood with his arms around the stone, feeling its coolness on his forehead. A fresh breeze caressed his hands on the other side of the stone.

He was headed someplace but didn't know where. The stone almost told him, but then the secret disappeared again. After a moment he could look around. The burial mounds appeared out of the darkness of the night, one after the other. Then they started rocking and turning on top of each other, and he leaned his head against the cool stone again. And after a moment, he knew where he was going. The cave opening that he wanted to crawl into. Inside, on the moss and the twigs, was deliverance.

After a while he could let go of the stone. He took a few steps, but the ground rose quickly before him, and he fell against the side of the mound. He kept crawling over a few mounds, up and down. Beyond a clump of trees on the shore the black water glistened. That's where he was headed.

He got to his feet again by the clump of trees. The trees were dense; he went from trunk to trunk, guiding himself down to the boat. It took a long time to get it away from shore, and he felt the water rising up his legs. Finally he sat by the oars, but his body burned like fire with every pull. He saw the mainland forest in jagged silhouette against the sky. He had to get there.

He rowed, his blood running off the seat and coloring the bilge water. He didn't notice. Once Ausi and Tora appeared to him, but they soon vanished. It was the cave that would save him.

The reeds were sparse and the water shallow where he reached the mainland. He toppled out of the boat and felt the cool, soothing water. He lay there a while and then crawled to shore. The boat stayed where he left it and would probably drift away, but he didn't have the strength even to think about that.

An older man, who was going out night-fishing, had watched the incoming boat for a moment. As the huge figure crawled splashing to land, got up, fell, and got up again, the old man's hair and beard stood up, too. With a whimper, he scampered away along the shore on his skinny legs. Holme hadn't seen him. He was following something that relentlessly guided him to his goal.

The chieftain and the Christian priests waited impatiently for the four warriors to return. But the night passed, and there was no sign of them. Across the courtyard, a sacrificial feast was in progress, but all the while the heathens kept a watch outside the hall.

Toward morning, the chieftain and one of the priests, with a couple of warriors for protection, went to find out what was going on. They walked in the direction where something had to have happened. They soon found a figure lying still, face down. The warriors were angry when they saw that he was one of their own men.

The other three were not far away. But the one they longed to see wasn't there. The chieftain and the priest looked at each other in silent horror. Was there nothing that could be done against that thrall? He had to be Satan himself.

They soon found the trail of blood and followed it. Maybe he had received a fatal wound in the fight after all. The blood extended all the way to the pebbles on the shore. He must have had the strength to row, even though masses of his blood had been spilled on the ground.

The Christians turned back and began praying in their hearts that their enemy might die from his wounds. Maybe they should send boats out to look for him. He must have rowed home to the king's farmstead.

But when the chieftain and the priests talked with the warriors about that, they grimly shook their heads. They walked out instead after their dead companions. Two of them had been cut down by an ax; the other two had been crushed or beaten to death at the thrall's hand.

Before the altar, the priests prayed for their god to search out and destroy the evil creature wherever he might be. Humans were powerless against him. They also asked Christ to receive the souls of the four warriors. He should destroy the heathens across from them who wouldn't be baptized, too. As Christ knew, this was the land lone in the north that wouldn't relinquish its heathen gods. Stubbornly and ruthlessly, they held fast to the bloody wooden idols.

Then the chieftain and priests decided to wait and see what happened. As long as the heathens didn't know about Holme, there was no danger. They would undoubtedly wait days for his return.

Svein had no peace while Holme was away. He didn't drink beer like the others, but several times he walked out and looked in a certain direction. He tried to sleep once, but the bench was hard, and the thralls were making noise around him.

At daybreak, he was out again. He was going to walk to the shore this time to look across the lake. Maybe Holme was already rowing back in the dawn with his wife and daughter. He heard some people coming toward him and hid quickly in a thicket. It wasn't so certain that peace reigned outside the temple, if they were Christians who were coming.

What he saw made him wonder at first if a battle raged on another part of the island. Several warriors came up the path carrying their dead comrades. One, two, three, four. Austerely they looked straight ahead, no one saying a word. When their steps had died away, Svein walked on.

Only upon reaching the shore did it occur to him what must have happened. He saw the trail of blood and a pair of large footprints that he knew well. He was filled with pride and joy. Four warriors had lain in wait, but Holme had killed all of them and could still continue on his way. There was a lot of blood, but he would surely be all right, just like always.

He ran back and reported everything to the heathen priests. The free thrall flew into a rage and wanted immediate revenge, but the priests calmed him down. They had to look for Holme first and find out if he was all right.

Svein immediately offered to go and took a couple of strong thralls with him to row the boat. The free thrall had to stay to take Holme's place if the Christians decided to attack. He was satisfied with that, shook his ax, and glared threateningly at the Christian church.

Ausi saw the boat in the distance. She had almost expected it; something had kept her awake all night. She felt that something was imminent, something conclusive. Maybe the end of life.

She woke Tora, and they walked to the shore. Tora, not noticing her anxiety, waited with curiosity. She soon saw, to her disappointment, that her father wasn't in the boat. But then her eyes started sparkling, and she avoided her mother's glance.

A few boat lengths from land, Svein yelled out to ask how Holme was. Mother and daughter looked at each other with silent terror; it was as if a hand had ripped at their hearts and they couldn't speak. Meanwhile, the boat landed and Svein hurried up to them. He saw at once that they knew nothing about Holme.

The women stepped silently into the boat, and the men rowed back without a word. A window opened in the king's house and someone watched them go.

Ausi already knew more than anyone else, and she wasn't thinking much about Holme now. But she looked at Tora and noticed Svein, who kept looking at the girl's bowed head the whole time. His eyes were good and honest; he would surely protect her. Besides, Tora could protect herself better than any other woman. She was courageous, impetuous, and strong. Her father's love for freedom lived in her, and she could never be a thrall to anyone.

Svein said something about Holme's possibly returning to town, but Ausi shook her head and pointed toward the mainland forest. After some hesitation, Svein motioned for the oarsmen to row there. A calm strength streamed from Ausi, and he felt that he must do as she said. She stared constantly in one direction and seemed to have forgotten about everyone else in the boat.

When she stepped ashore, she looked at Tora and Svein for a moment. But they had said they would follow her wherever she went. When she saw that in their eyes, she walked toward the forest, and they followed her at a little distance. The oarsmen watched them and then rowed off toward town: they were curious about what was going on back there, and they were also longing for the good, strong beer.

The three of them walked nearly all day. Sometimes they would stop, and Tora looked wonderingly at her mother. Her face seemed normal; she was just more beautiful and somehow distant from them. She seemed to be listening for something and had no peace.

Svein took Tora's hand as often as he dared, and she let him hold it. A couple of times he also got a friendly, searching look and a smile. His heart was full of that singular happiness, and he didn't think at all about Holme.

In the sunset, they saw the ridge were the cave was. Svein didn't know about the cave, and he looked in surprise at the dark opening. Outside lay several things, thrown from the cave – a sledgehammer, an ax, a hammer, tongs, drill bits, a saw, and a scythe.

Ausi signaled for the young people to stop, then got down on her knees and crawled into the cave. They heard her talking and whispering tenderly inside, so they sat down on the mossy boulder outside and waited hand in hand.

When Ausi came out she said quietly that Holme was in there, and that no one would ever see him outside the cave again. She would stay with him. She was his wife and had a right to do that.

Tora and Svein looked at her in silence. They could hear and see that talking would do no good. Ausi's face was radiant and clear, but she looked at them as if from a great distance. She said, too, that Holme had thrown the tools out so they could be of use to someone else. That's how he'd always been.

They should go on now and not worry about her. If they wanted to close up the cave with stones afterward, that would be good. Otherwise, wild animals would find their way in.

And the young people soon walked on. Tora didn't cry, but she kept turning around. Her mother, stately and beautiful, stood on the ridge watching them. Tora knew that she would never see either of her parents again, but she walked away calmly. Svein's hand was numbed by her hard grip, and her tears fell quietly in the moss. He was thinking she was Holme's daughter, and he smiled proudly. For generations people would talk about Holme, his wife Ausi, and their daughter, who was Svein's woman.

When Ausi couldn't see them any more, she went back to the cave. She moved calmly and with dignity as she broke off branches to cover the opening a little until it could be shut up with stones again. She talked out loud into the cave as she did so.

When she was through, Ausi looked around. She thought about the morning when Holme came running and dragged her with him to the cave after saving Tora from a wild animal's jaws. The memory of how much she had feared him made her smile.

She hadn't known then that the silent and feared thrall was the finest man alive.

Thoughts swarmed inside her, but Ausi couldn't let them out yet. She didn't want to make Holme wait too long. She dragged the branches within reach, looked around again, and crawled inside. The massive figure lay quiet and still inside, his face peaceful in the darkness. She lay down beside him, tenderly lifting his heavy, still head, and putting her supple arm under his neck. She ran her other hand over his body and soon found what she was looking for. The knife blade shone dully in the sparse light coming in through the cave opening. She didn't have to check to see if the knife was sharp. Holme never carried a tool or weapon that wasn't sharp and strong.

But Ausi still had one more thing to do, the most important thing of all. She had to talk with Christ so that He would be prepared when she and Holme came to Him. She was certain that He would understand and receive them well. He could also see them here in the cave – something a wooden god surely never could have done. Holme hadn't had water poured on his head, and the priests said that without that a person couldn't reach Christ and have things good. . . .

A thought made Ausi carefully withdraw her arm and crawl out of the cave. She hurried along the slope to the spring, and a squirrel chattered angrily at her from the top of a spruce tree. She filled her hands with the cold spring water and returned to the cave. She crawled in carefully, raised her cupped hands over Holme's head, thought for a moment, and then said out loud, 'Oh, Christ, now I baptize my husband in Your name so that he can follow along with me to You. He is much better than anyone else, more like You than Your priests are. We'll be coming soon.' She thought a little more and added, 'Better, except for the one You sent here first.'

Satisfied and happy, she resumed her position, feeling the water on Holme's head moistening her arm. Everything was ready. There was plenty of time to talk with Christ about Tora once they got to Him. She was in good hands until then.

She had laid the knife on Holme's chest and now groped for it again. She wondered where Holme's fatal wound was – she'd like to stab herself in the same place. But she didn't want to change positions again, so instead moved only her upper body so she could get her arm and hand away from Holme's head. She aimed the knife and drove it in. The warmth gushed over her hand, and she smiled contentedly as she lay back down.

She realized that she had forgotten to pull the branches in front of the opening. Well, that did no harm; the young people would come back soon.

It got darker and darker in the cave, and soon she no longer had any feeling in her body. A pleasant fatigue engulfed her, and she wanted to fall asleep. But it soon passed, and the cave got lighter. The light intensified quickly, and she could see through the cave wall. Could it be Christ on His way to them?

It was early morning now, exactly like the first time. The stones on the slope bore light yellow stripes that faded away in the light around them. Butterflies fluttered about, and the water from the spring glistened brightly. There was still something alien about the scene, however, and she was a little frightened. She was still so alone.

At that instant, she saw Holme standing outside the cave. His face was peaceful, full of love, and younger than when he had fought in town. He looked warmly and tenderly at her, and she flew jubilantly into his arms. She felt herself enclosed by his arms, and then he carried her away over grass, flowers, and butterflies. She heard him say something about her needing to rest first. Then she would learn something very important and very pleasant.

After a couple of days had passed and Holme had not returned, the chieftain and priests began to hope that he had been fatally wounded. They also saw many signs of uneasiness among the heathens. They walked out often, looking across the water toward the king's farmstead and the mainland forest, and finally they sent messages to many places. The Christians saw the messengers return without success.

Svein's mother rejoiced with them, although she noticed uneasily that her son could no longer be seen at the heathen temple. She must be certain about his fate. And so she decided to go to the relatives' farmstead to look for him. The chieftain reluctantly gave her a couple of older men for help and protection on the journey.

She noticed from a distance that there were people at the farmstead. She was happy again, thinking that now she would return to town just once more, and then only to find out about Holme's wife and daughter. They were her thralls, and she would make sure they knew it.

The thought got her worked up, and she walked toward the new building without paying any attention to the men who were finishing up the work there. She didn't ask about her son but walked straight in through the door. From the hearth, she was met by a pair of surprised black eyes and she herself stopped in amazement when she realized it was the thrall's daughter. Svein's mother let loose an angry, triumphant hissing sound and rushed forward. Before Tora had time to react, she felt the older woman's hand in her hair.

But not for long. Svein's mother saw the dark eyes flash and felt a strong hand grab her wrist. When she felt the grip she remembered in the midst of her rage whose daughter it was. Her arm was twisted now so that her fingers lost their hold, and a sudden jerk cast her to the floor.

The men outside heard the racket but didn't have time to look in before the older woman came bounding out. Holme's daughter was chasing her, dancing a bundle of birch twigs off her back and head. They ran down the slope, the men laughing loudly and raucously as they went.

Tora returned soon, and the men praised her and talked about whose daughter she was. She was still furious, but that soon passed, and she smiled at the men, her white teeth glistening as she walked back into the house.

Just then, Svein came down out of the woods, and he saw a bowed figure on his father's burial mound. He stopped in surprise, but the men waved to him and laughingly told him what had just happened. They praised Holme's daughter and warned him kiddingly about provoking her.

He walked proudly and happily into the house but met a gaze that made him stop for a moment. The look asked angrily and proudly on whose side he was in this fight between the women. This was soon made clear to Holme's daughter. Svein stroked her hair with love, pride, and respect. For the first time she put her arms around him, and he lost his breath for a moment. She pressed against him, and he thought happily about a moment that would have to come soon. He also sensed that the look and those arms were like Holme's. Svein had to be either with her or against her. Although she was a woman, it could still be dangerous to be against her. The bowed figure on his father's burial mound witnessed to that. He knew that his mother's role had been played out, and he was glad.

A late summer cloud passed over the town on the island; the warring parties dispersed again without resolving the conflict, and the grinning wooden gods looked across at the Christian church. The Christian priests would flee this rugged land yet again, and what they called the heathen darkness would hover over it for a hundred years more.[14]

Like two trails of blood, Christendom and the fight for freedom would proceed through the centuries side by side. The town would be destroyed, and for centuries, no one would know where it had been.[15] But the two trails that originated there have still not, a thousand years later, reached their destination.

14. The mission efforts of Ansgar and his successors are considered a mere episode, having little impact on Swedish history. Archbishop Unni of Hamburg renewed the mission in about 936, but likewise met with brief and questionable success. Unni died in Birka, perhaps by stoning, on September 17, 936, "the first precise date we know for domestic Swedish history" (Franklin D. Scott, *Sweden: The Nation's History* [Minneapolis: Univ. of Minnesota Press, 1977], p. 35). See also Ingvar Andersson, *A History of Sweden*, trans. Carolyn Hannay (New York: Praeger, 1956), p. 26.

15. Birka essentially vanished at the end of the tenth century and was not rediscovered until the end of the seventeenth. See Birgit Arrhenius, ed., *Ansgars Birka* (Stockholm: P. A. Norstedts & Söner, 1965).

Selected Bibliography

Translations

Fridegård, Jan. *I, Lars Hård* (*Jag Lars Hård*, 1935). Translated, with an introduction and notes, by Robert E. Bjork. Lincoln and London: University of Nebraska Press, 1983.

——. *Jacob's Ladder* (*Tack för himlastegen*, 1936) and *Mercy* (*Barmhärtighet*, 1936). Translated, with introductions and notes, by Robert E. Bjork. Lincoln and London: University of Nebraska Press, 1985.

——. "The Key" ("Nyckeln," 1944). Translated by Robert E. Bjork. *Translation: The Journal of Literary Translation* 15 (1985): 270–75.

——. *Land of Wooden Gods* (*Trägudars land*, 1940). Translated, with an afterword and notes, by Robert E. Bjork. Lincoln and London: University of Nebraska Press, 1989.

——. "Natural Selection" ("Det naturliga urvalet," 1939). Translated by Robert E. Bjork. *Malahat Review* 55 (1980): 104–10.

——. "1987 Translation Prize Selection from *Land of Wooden Gods*." Translated by Robert E. Bjork. *Scandinavian Review* 76, no. 4 (1988): 77–82.

——. "100 Kilos Rye" ("Kvarnbudet," 1944). Translated by Robert E. Bjork. *Scandinavian Review* 68, no. 2 (1980): 54–62.

——. *People of the Dawn* (*Gryningsfolket*, 1944). Translated, with a foreword and notes, by Robert E. Bjork. Lincoln and London: University of Nebraska Press, 1990.

Criticism

Gamby, Erik. *Jan Fridegård. Introduktion till ett författarskap.* Stockholm: Svenska bokförlaget, 1956.

Graves, Peter. *Jan Fridegård: Lars Hård.* Studies in Swedish Literature, no. 8. Hull: University of Hull, 1977. (In English.)

Lundkvist, Artur, and Lars Forssell, eds. *Jan Fridegård.* Stockholm: Förlaget frilansen, 1949.

Schön, Ebbe. *Jan Fridegård och forntiden. En studie i diktverk och källor.* Uppsala, Sweden: Almqvist & Wiksell, 1973.

——. *Jan Fridegård. Proletärdiktaren och folkkulturen.* Stockholm: Wahlström & Widstrand, 1978.